The Adventures of
PINOCCHIO

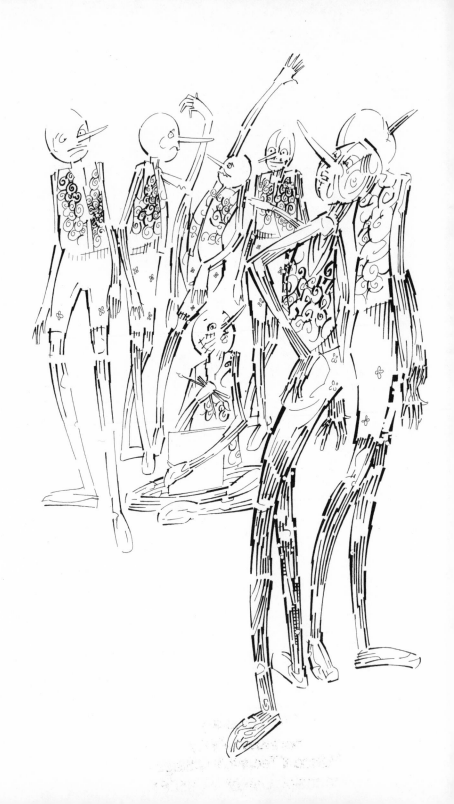

The Adventures of
PINOCCHIO

Story of a Puppet

Carlo Collodi

TRANSLATED BY NANCY CANEPA

ILLUSTRATIONS BY CARMELO LETTERE

STEERFORTH ITALIA

AN IMPRINT OF STEERFORTH PRESS · SOUTH ROYALTON, VERMONT

For information about permission to reproduce
selections from this book, write to:
Steerforth Press L.C., P.O. Box 70,
South Royalton, Vermont 05068

Library of Congress Cataloging-in-Publication Data

Collodi, Carlo, 1826–1890.
  [Avventure di Pinocchio. English]
  Pinocchio : story of a puppet / Carlo Collodi ; translated by Nancy Canepa ;
illustrations by Carmelo Lettere. — 1st ed.
     p.   cm.
  ISBN 1-58642-052-6 (alk. paper)
  I. Canepa, Nancy L., 1957– II. Lettere, Carmelo. III. Title.
PQ4712.L4 A713 2002
853'.8—dc21   2002009081

FIRST EDITION

A
Gaia e Camilla

*T*HE STORY OF Pinocchio — the rascally puppet who, through experience, comes to realize the advantages of mending his ways and becomes a "decent" flesh-and-blood boy — is today familiar and beloved the world over. In Italy, Pinocchio is a national hero, and the novel that recounts his feats, Carlo Collodi's *The Adventures of Pinocchio* (1881–83), is among the most influential works of modern Italian literature. It has appeared in more than two hundred translations in over a hundred languages, including Latin. A similarly large number of artists have tried their hands at illustrating the tale, and it has seen many movie versions, the best-known Disney's 1940 animation and the most recent a live-action film starring and directed by Roberto Benigni. There have been rewritings — *A Comment on the Life of Pinocchio*, *The Return of Pinocchio*, and so forth — and theatrical and musical adaptations, such as Carmelo Bene's 1962 dramatization. One of Italy's pop successes of the 1970s was the album by Edoardo Bennato entitled *Burattino senza fili* (Puppet without Strings), entirely dedicated to Pinocchio and his fellow characters.

Characters and episodes from *Pinocchio* are routinely used as points of reference in discussions of current events in Italian newspapers, and over the past several decades studies and conferences dedicated to Collodi's book have proliferated. Italy's great literary critic and historian Benedetto Croce once commented that "[t]he wood from which Pinocchio is carved is Humanity itself." The vitality of Collodi's novel seems as boundless as that of the puppet who dreamed of becoming a real boy, and readers of all ages still delight in a tale that, though firmly rooted in the humus of the nineteenth-century Tuscan countryside, speaks to all of us of the pull between childlike freedom and creativity on the one hand and maturity and social responsibility on the other. As such, it will never lose its irresistible appeal.

Pinocchio's creator, Carlo Collodi, was born Carlo Lorenzini in Florence, Italy, in 1826. His parents were of humble origin — his father served as a cook for a noble Florentine family — and began their lives in the nearby village of Collodi, from which Lorenzini later took his pen name. Although educated primarily in religious institutions, he rebelled against a career in the church. As a young man in 1848, and then again in 1859, he fought for Italy's independence in the long struggle known as the Risorgimento. For a good part of his life Collodi worked as a civil servant, but he was also a fairly well-known journalist and writer. He served on the editorial staff of the Florentine newspaper *Il Fanfulla* and was later involved in the important children's magazine *Il Giornale dei bambini*, whose first issue appeared in 1881. In addition to *The Adventures of Pinocchio*, Collodi's published works include collections of his newspaper articles, several other children's books, and a translation of classic French fairy tales. Collodi died in 1890, several years after the death of his beloved mother, with whom he lived, never having married himself.

And then there is *Pinocchio*, the reason Collodi's name is familiar today. The first fifteen chapters were first published in serialized form as *Storia di un burattino* (Story of a Puppet) in *Il Giornale dei bambini* (The Children's Journal), from July 1881 to January 1883. Although Collodi originally intended to end his tale with Pinocchio left for dead, hanging on the Great Oak, the clamor on the part of his "little readers" made him reconsider. And so Pinocchio was revived, and a second part of his tale written, *Le avventure di Pinocchio* (The Adventures of Pinocchio). In early 1883 the Florentine publisher Paggi issued the entire book under the name *Le avventure di Pinocchio: Storia di un burattino*, with pen-and-ink illustrations by Enrico Mazzanti. Before Collodi died, four more editions followed, in 1886, 1887, 1888, and 1890. The title was eventually condensed to *Le avventure di Pinocchio.*

During Collodi's lifetime children's literature was a relatively new development, as was the idea that childhood was a period unto itself, governed by its own rules and deserving its own culture. Many factors were responsible for this change, including the rise of the middle class, growing literacy among children, mandatory schooling, and changing concepts of leisure time. Also important were the emergence of folklore studies earlier in the nineteenth century and the publication of fairy-tale collections such as the Brothers Grimm's *Children's and Household Tales* (1812) and Hans Christian Andersen's *Fairy Tales* (1835). Indeed, the period spanning the last decades of the nineteenth century and the first of the twentieth has often been labeled the "golden age" of children's literature for its string of classics, including Lewis Carroll's *Alice in Wonderland* (1865) and *Through the Looking Glass* (1872), L. Frank Baum's *The Wizard of Oz* (1900), J. M. Barrie's *Peter Pan* (1904), and, of course, Collodi's *Pinocchio.*

At first glance *Pinocchio* might appear to conform to the requisites of the pedagogical novel intended to mold children into ideal little citizens, a popular vehicle for offering instruction on appropriate socialization at a time of European nation-building. But that is only part of the story. Like a fairy tale, *Pinocchio* recounts a journey of initiation fraught with obstacles that culminates with the rebirth of the hero into adulthood. It adopts the common fairy-tale motifs of a fairy godmother, talking animals, magical helpers and antagonists, and other marvelous beings. Yet it also has much in common with more realistic genres. The social world in which Pinocchio moves is colored by privation, violence, and indifference, and the message that is constantly drummed into him — that the only way to achieve social validation is through hard work, self-reliance, and obedience to one's superiors — is not exactly the enchanted "happily-ever-after" of fairy tales. In the end *Pinocchio*'s appeal lies in the rich diversity of traditions and visions upon which it draws.

This often surprising interplay between the fantastic and the real is evident right from the first lines of the first chapter:

> Once upon a time there was . . .
> "A king!" my little readers will immediately say.
> No, children, you're wrong. Once upon a time there
> was a piece of wood.

It is clear that although the tale may begin with "once upon a time," conventional fairy-tale expectations won't be met. When the wood speaks later in this same chapter, the marvelous makes its first appearance, and the stage is set for a tale of initiation populated by fantastic creatures and impoverished Tuscan peasants and featuring as its protagonist a talking puppet who at times seems blessed by fortune, at others the victim of grim reality. The animals that populate *Pinocchio* are less magical creatures than allegorical projections of human types: the Cat and the Fox are con-men incarnate; the Talking Cricket is a self-righteous proselytizer. The hardships in Pinocchio's world are relentless. His few moments of physical content are punctuated by regular bouts with hunger, cold, and the risk of death, and he is ever in search of a place where, in his words, "one can eat without running the risk of being eaten." The human landscape that Pinocchio traverses is no less desolate. Its inhabitants, from hard-hearted peasants to vision-impaired judges, again and again prove devious, cold and unsympathetic, even perverse. Nor can Pinocchio's "family" guarantee a consistently secure haven from the harsh outside world. Geppetto and the Blue Fairy do show love and concern, yet they too can be cruel and selfish.

Collodi's moral vision is fundamentally ambivalent. The desirability of joining the human, or adult, world is hammered into Pinocchio from the beginning to the end of the book. But this is a profoundly unjust and corrupt world; we may well ask ourselves if adapting to it, as Pinocchio inevitably does, means extinguishing what is most human and humane in him. There is no doubt that Pinocchio is a scamp and that children — and adults — must grow up, rein in their instincts, and compromise their creativity in order to live in society. But it is also true that the free-spirited Pinocchio has a kind heart and sense of justice, and it is because of these, in the end, that readers love him. Pinocchio's lasting attraction has much less to do with the puppet's metamorphosis into a responsible member of society than with the unleashed vitality of which he gives constant and poignant proof, and we can only wonder if the new, "respectable" Pinocchio will have much chance to cultivate his best qualities in his life as a boy. The last image of the transformed Pinocchio, who complacently observes the lifeless puppet, is somehow disquieting, because Pinocchio's struggle between transgression and conformity, between being a bad boy and a good boy, sums up the instinctive anxieties that we all feel about "growing up" and encourages us to reflect, finally, upon just who the puppets really are.

NANCY CANEPA

COLLODI ONCE DECLARED: "I'm one who writes the same way I talk." Collodi's "simple" style is, in fact, fruit of a linguistic and rhetorical mastery that is far from any spontaneous naïveté. The light elegance of *Pinocchio* results from the playful balance its author is able to sustain between the simulation of oral storytelling and a more self-consciously literary voice. In my translation I have aimed, above all, to replicate this marvelous agility. When this has meant veering from the path of a literal translation (in any case often a dangerous one), I have done so. I used the Italian critical edition of Ornella Castellani Pollidori that was published during the 1983 Pinocchio centennial by the Fondazione Nazionale Carlo Collodi.

The Adventures of
PINOCCHIO

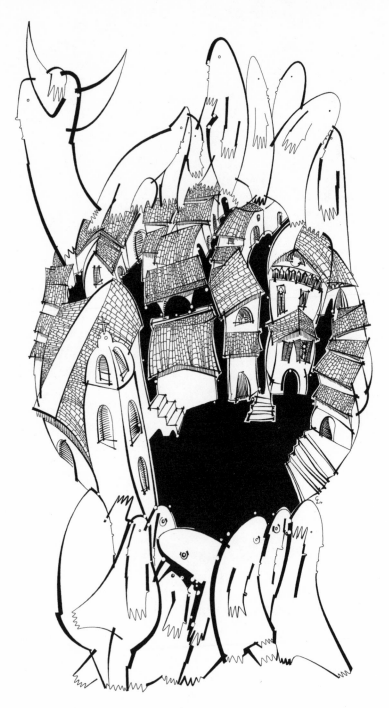

C'era una volta . . . "Un re!" diranno subito i miei
piccoli lettori. "No, ragazzi, avete sbagliato."

CHAPTER ONE

**How it happened that Master Cherry,
a carpenter, found a piece of wood
that cried and laughed like a child.**

*O*NCE UPON A time there was . . .

"A king!" my little readers will immediately say.

No, children, you're wrong. Once upon a time there was a piece of wood.

It wasn't anything valuable, just a simple piece of wood that you might find on a wood pile, of the sort that you put in woodstoves and fireplaces in the winter to heat your rooms.

I don't know how it happened, but the fact of the matter is that one fine day this piece of wood turned up in the workshop of an old carpenter, whose name was Master Antonio, although everyone called him Master Cherry on account of the tip of his nose, which was always shiny and purplish, like a ripe cherry.

As soon as Master Cherry saw that piece of wood he grew quite cheerful, and, rubbing his hands with happiness, he mumbled under his breath:

"This wood has turned up just at the right moment; I think I'll use it to make a table leg."

No sooner said than done: he got his sharpened ax and prepared to remove the bark and whittle down the wood. But just as he was about to strike the first blow he stopped, with his arm hanging in the air, because he heard a tiny, thin little voice that said beseechingly:

"Don't hit me so hard!"

Imagine how surprised that fine old Master Cherry was!

His bewildered eyes roamed the room, trying to discover just where that little voice could have come from, but he saw no one! He looked under the bench: no one; he looked in a cupboard that was always kept closed: no one; he looked in the basket where he put wood shavings and sawdust: no one; he opened the door of his workshop and had a look at the street, too: no one. Well, then?

"I see," he said then, laughing and scratching his wig, "I clearly must have imagined that little voice. Let's get back to work now."

And he picked up the hatchet again and struck the piece of wood with an almighty blow.

"Ouch! You hurt me!" the same little voice yelled out in complaint.

This time Master Cherry was left speechless. His eyes bulged out of his head with fear, his mouth fell wide open, and his tongue dangled down to his chin; he looked just like a gargoyle on a fountain.

As soon as he was able to form words again, he began to speak, shaking and stuttering with fright:

"But where can that little voice that said *ouch* have come from? . . . After all, there's not a living soul here. Could it be this piece of wood that has learned to cry and complain like a little child? I can't believe it. Let's have a look at this wood here: it's a piece of firewood, the same as any other; throw it on the fire and it'll boil a pot of beans . . . Well, then? Could someone be hiding inside of it? If someone is hiding in there, so much the worse for him. I'll take care of him now!"

And as he said this he grabbed that poor piece of wood with both hands and began to slam it without mercy against the walls of the room.

Then he stopped to listen, to hear if a little voice would start complaining. He waited two minutes: nothing; five minutes: nothing; ten minutes: nothing!

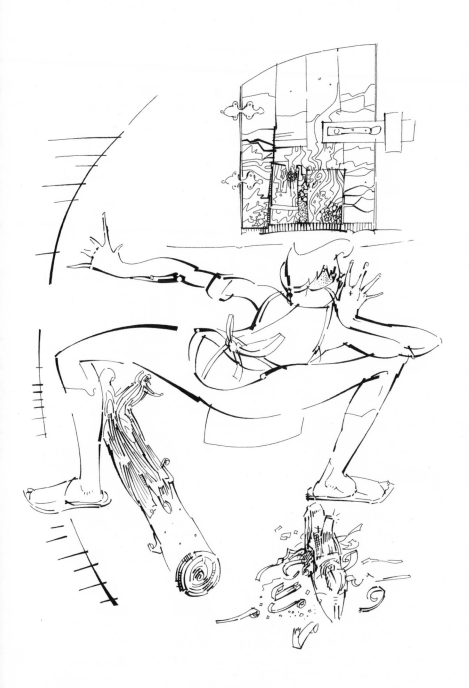

. . . una vocina . . .

"I see," he said, then, forcing himself to laugh and ruffling his wig, "I clearly must have imagined that little voice that said *ouch!* Let's get back to work now."

And since a great fear had come over him, he tried singing a tune under his breath to work up some courage.

In the meantime he put his hatchet to one side and took up his plane, intending to plane and polish the piece of wood, but while he was planing it up and down he heard the same little voice say to him, laughing:

"Stop! You're tickling my stomach!"

This time poor Master Cherry fell down as if he had been struck by lightning. When he opened his eyes again, he found himself sitting on the ground.

His face appeared disfigured, and even the tip of his nose, which was almost always purplish, had become blue from the great fright he had had.

CHAPTER TWO

**Master Cherry gives the piece of wood to his
friend Geppetto, who takes it with the
intention of making a marvelous puppet
that can dance, fence, and do flips.**

*J*UST THEN THERE was a knock on the door.
"Come on in," said the carpenter, without having the
strength to get to his feet.

And then into the workshop came a sprightly little old man
whose name was Geppetto, although when the neighborhood
boys wanted to drive him crazy they called him by the nickname
of Polendina, because of his yellow wig, which looked very much
like corn polenta.

Geppetto was quite a cantankerous fellow. God forbid you
called him Polendina! He would turn right into a wild beast, and
then there was no restraining him.

"Good day, Master Antonio," said Geppetto. "What are you
doing on the ground there?"

"I'm teaching the ants some arithmetic."

"Much good may it do you!"

"What brought you here, Geppetto my friend?"

"My legs. You should know, Master Antonio, that I've come to
ask you a favor."

"Here I am, ready to serve you," replied the carpenter, getting
up on his knees.

"This morning I had a brainstorm."

"Let's hear."

"I thought I'd make myself a nice wooden puppet — a marvelous puppet, one that can dance, fence, and do flips. I intend to go all over the world with this puppet and earn my crust of bread and glass of wine by him. What do you think?"

"Bravo, Polendina!" shouted the same little voice that was coming from who knows where.

When he heard himself called Polendina, Master Geppetto got as red as a pepper with rage and, turning toward the carpenter, said to him furiously:

"Why are you insulting me?"

"Who's insulting you?"

"You called me Polendina!"

"It wasn't me."

"That's right; it must have been me! I say it was you."

"No!"

"Yes!"

"No!"

"Yes!"

And as they got more and more fired up, they passed from words to actions, and then they started to fight, scratching, biting, and tearing each other up.

When the battle was over, Master Antonio found Geppetto's yellow wig in his hands, and Geppetto realized that he had the carpenter's grayish one in his mouth.

"Give me back my wig!" shouted Master Antonio.

"And you give me back mine, and then we'll make up."

After each of them had gotten back his own wig, the two little old men shook hands and swore they'd stay good friends for the rest of their lives.

"So, Geppetto, my friend," said the carpenter in sign of the peace they had made, "what's the favor you want to ask me?"

"I'd like a little bit of wood so that I can make my puppet. Will you give me some?"

"Polendina!"

Master Antonio, quite pleased, went straight to his workbench to get that piece of wood that had given him such a fright. But just as he was about to hand it over to his friend, the piece of wood gave a sudden jerk, wriggled violently out of his hands, and finally went banging against poor Geppetto's scrawny shins.

"Ah! So this is the polite way you give away your things, Master Antonio? You almost crippled me!"

"I swear it wasn't me!"

"Then it must have been me!"

"It's all this piece of wood's fault . . ."

"I know that it's the wood's fault, but you're the one who threw it at my legs!"

"It wasn't me who threw it!"

"Liar!"

"Don't insult me, Geppetto, or else I'll call you Polendina!"

"Ass!"

"Polendina!"

"Donkey!"

"Polendina!"

"Ugly old ape!"

"Polendina!"

When he heard himself called Polendina for the third time, Geppetto was blinded by rage and went for the carpenter, and right then and there they beat the tar out of each other.

When the battle was over, Master Antonio found himself with two new scratches on his nose, and the other fellow with two fewer buttons on his jacket. After they had squared their accounts in this way they shook hands and swore they'd stay good friends for the rest of their lives.

And finally, Geppetto took his dear piece of wood, and after thanking Master Antonio he limped back home.

CHAPTER THREE

**After returning home, Geppetto immediately
starts making the puppet and gives him the
name of Pinocchio. The puppet's first mischief.**

GEPPETTO'S HOUSE WAS a little room on the ground
floor, which got its light from a stairwell. The furnishings
couldn't have been simpler: a battered chair, a dilapidated bed,
and a broken-down little table. On the back wall you could see a
fireplace with a fire burning, but the fire was painted, and near
the fire there was painted a pot that boiled cheerfully and sent
forth a cloud of steam that looked just like real steam.

As soon as he entered the house, Geppetto immediately took
up his tools and started to carve and shape his puppet.

"What name shall I give him?" he asked himself. "I'll call him
Pinocchio; that name will bring him good luck. Once I knew an
entire family of Pinocchios: the father was a Pinocchio, the mother
was a Pinocchia, and the children were Pinocchios, and they all
managed pretty well. The richest of them was a beggar."

When he had found a name for his puppet, he began to work
seriously, and he quickly made the hair, then the forehead, then
the eyes.

Once the eyes were done, imagine his astonishment when he
realized that they were moving and staring at him intently.

When he saw those two wooden eyes staring at him, Geppetto
felt a bit offended and said in a resentful tone:

"You nasty wooden eyes, why are you looking at me?"

No one answered.

And so after the eyes, he made the puppet a nose, but as soon as the nose was done it started to grow. And it grew, and grew, and grew, and in a few minutes it had become so long that you could barely see the end of it.

Poor Geppetto wore himself out trying to cut it back, but the more he chopped at it and tried to cut it down, the longer that impertinent nose became.

After the nose, he made the puppet a mouth.

The mouth wasn't even finished when it started right up laughing and making fun of Geppetto.

"Cut out that laughing!" said Geppetto in a huff, but it was like talking to the wall.

"Cut out that laughing, I said!" he shouted in a threatening voice.

At that the mouth stopped laughing, but it stuck out its entire tongue.

Geppetto pretended not to notice so that he wouldn't ruin what he was doing and continued to work. After the mouth he made the chin, then the neck, then the shoulders, the stomach, the arms, and the hands.

As soon as he had finished the hands, Geppetto felt his wig being taken off his head. He looked up, and what did he see? He saw his yellow wig in the hands of the puppet.

"Pinocchio! . . . Give me back my wig this minute!"

But instead of giving him back the wig, Pinocchio put it on his own head and was nearly smothered by it.

At that insolent and derisive conduct, Geppetto became more sad and melancholy than he had ever been in his life, and, turning to Pinocchio, he said:

"You scamp of a child! You're not even finished, and you're already starting to be disrespectful to your father! That's bad, my boy, bad!"

And he dried off a tear.

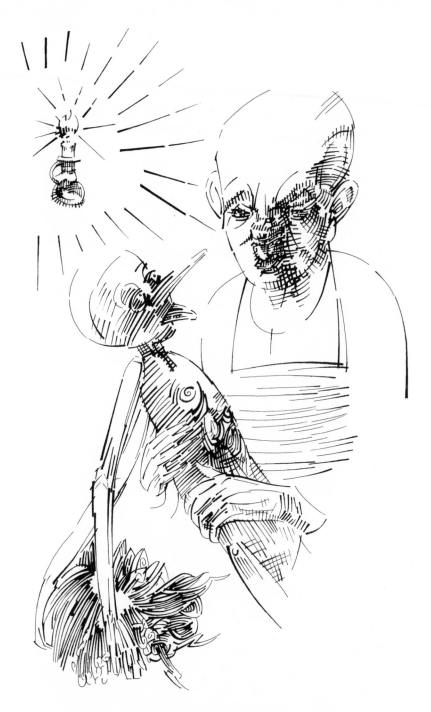

"Pinocchio! . . . rendimi subito la mia parrucca!"

The legs and the feet still remained to be made.

When Geppetto had finished making the feet, he felt a kick land on the tip of his nose.

"I deserve this!" he said to himself then. "I should have thought of this before! It's too late now!"

Then he took hold of the puppet under the arms and placed him down on the floor of the room, so that he could start walking.

Pinocchio's legs were stiff and he didn't know how to move, so Geppetto led him by the hand and taught him how to take one step after the other.

Once he had stretched his legs, Pinocchio started to walk by himself and then to run around the room, until finally he slipped out the door, jumped into the street, and started to run away.

Poor Geppetto ran after him but wasn't able to reach him, because that naughty Pinocchio went leaping along like a hare, and the beating of his wooden feet on the pavement of the street made as much racket as twenty pairs of peasants' clogs.

"Get him! Get him!" shouted Geppetto, but when the people in the street saw that wooden puppet running along like a race-horse they stopped in amazement to stare at him, and they laughed and laughed and laughed so hard that it was beyond all imagination.

At last — and lucky it was — a carabiniere happened to pass by. When he heard all the uproar he thought that perhaps a colt had broken away from its master, and he planted himself courageously in the middle of the street with his legs wide apart, his mind set on stopping it and preventing any greater mishaps from happening.

But when from a distance Pinocchio caught sight of the carabiniere, who was barricading the whole street, he came up with the bright idea of surprising him by slipping between his legs. It was, however, a fiasco.

Without budging an inch, the carabiniere caught him cleanly by the nose (and it was a huge nose, out of all proportion, which seemed to have been made for the express purpose of being

Il carabiniere, senza punto smuoversi,
lo acciuffò pulitamente per il naso . . .

grabbed by carabinieri) and delivered him back into the very hands of Geppetto, who, as punishment, intended to give the puppet's ears a good boxing as soon as he could. But imagine how he felt when he went to look for the ears and couldn't find them. And do you know why? Because in his great hurry to carve Pinocchio he had forgotten to make them.

So he grabbed him by the scruff of the neck, and as he was taking him back home he said, shaking his head threateningly:

"We're going home right now. And when we're home, you can rest assured that we'll settle our score!"

When he heard this sad tune, Pinocchio threw himself on the ground and refused to walk any farther. In the meantime, a crowd of busybodies and loafers began to gather around him.

There were those who said one thing, and those who said another.

"Poor puppet!" some said, "he's right not to want to go back home! Who knows what sort of a beating he may get from that brute Geppetto!"

And the others added maliciously:

"That Geppetto looks like a gentleman! But he's a real tyrant with children! If they leave that poor puppet in his hands, he's more than capable of smashing him to pieces!"

In short, they made such an uproar and such a commotion that the carabiniere set Pinocchio free and led poor Geppetto off to prison. And Geppetto, not coming up then and there with the right words to defend himself, started crying like a little calf, and as he went off to the jail, he stuttered through his sobs:

"Wretched boy! And to think how much I suffered to make him into a respectable puppet! But it serves me right! I should have thought of this before!"

What happened next is a story so strange that it's almost impossible to believe, and I'll tell you about it in the following chapters.

CHAPTER FOUR

**The story of Pinocchio and the Talking Cricket,
where it can be seen how bad boys resent being
corrected by those who know more than they do.**

J'LL TELL YOU THEN, children, that while poor Geppetto
was being taken off to prison through no fault of his own, that
rascal Pinocchio, once he had escaped the clutches of the carabiniere, took to his heels and started running through the fields so
he could get home faster. And in his great hurry, he jumped over
enormously high embankments, briar hedges, and ditches full of
water, just like a baby goat or hare might do if chased by hunters.

When he arrived in front of his house he found the street door
ajar. He pushed it open, went inside, and, as soon as he had bolted
the door shut, threw himself on the ground and just sat there, letting out a huge sigh of contentment.

But that contentment hadn't lasted very long before he heard
someone in the room go:

"Crick-crick-crick!"

"Who's calling me?" said Pinocchio, terrified.

"It is I!"

Pinocchio turned around and saw a large cricket climbing
slowly up the wall.

"Tell me, Cricket, who are you?"

"I am the Talking Cricket, and I have lived in this room for more than a hundred years."

"But now this room is mine," said the puppet, "and if you want to do me a real favor, get out of here right now, without a look behind you."

"I will not leave here," answered the Cricket, "if I do not first tell you a great truth."

"Tell me and be quick about it."

"Woe to those children who rebel against their parents and who abandon their homes to indulge their whims. They will never come to any good in this world, and sooner or later they will have to face a bitter repentance."

"Go ahead and sing as you will and wish, my dear Cricket. All I know is that tomorrow at dawn I'll be leaving, since if I stay here the same thing will happen to me that happens to every other child: I mean that they'll send me to school, and by hook or by crook I'll be forced to study, and — I'm telling you this confidentially — I don't have the slightest desire to study; I have more fun running after butterflies and climbing up trees to find baby birds."

"Poor little fool! Don't you know that if you do that you'll become a fine jackass when you grow up, and everyone will make fun of you?"

"Shut up, you nasty, bad-luck Cricket!" shouted Pinocchio.

But instead of taking offense at this impertinence, the Cricket, who was both patient and a philosopher, continued in the same tone of voice:

"And if you don't like the idea of going to school, why don't you at least learn a trade so that you can earn your bread honestly?"

"You want me to tell you?" replied Pinocchio, who was starting to lose his patience. "Of all the trades in the world there's only one that really appeals to me."

"And what trade would that be?"

"Eating, drinking, sleeping, having fun, and leading an idle life from morning till night."

"For your information," said the Talking Cricket with his usual

"Bada, Grillaccio . . ."

calm, "those who practice that trade almost always end up either in the hospital or in jail."

"Watch out, you nasty, bad-luck Cricket! . . . If I lose my temper, you'll be in trouble!"

"Poor Pinocchio! I really pity you!"

"Why do you pity me?"

"Because you're a puppet, and even worse, because you have a wooden head."

At these last words Pinocchio jumped up in a great fury, grabbed a wooden hammer from the workbench, and hurled it at the Talking Cricket.

Perhaps he didn't even think it would hit him, but, unfortunately, it got him right on the head, so that the poor Cricket hardly had the breath to say crick-crick-crick before he ended up perfectly dead and stuck to the wall.

CHAPTER FIVE

**Pinocchio is hungry and looks for an egg so
that he can make himself an omelet, but just as
he's about to eat it the omelet flies out the window.**

*I*N THE MEANTIME night began to fall, and Pinocchio, remembering that he hadn't eaten a thing, felt a little pang in
his stomach that quite closely resembled an appetite.

But a child's appetite makes quick progress, and in fact, after a
few minutes his appetite became hunger, and in the bat of an eye
the hunger was transformed into a wolfish craving, into a hunger
so thick you could cut it with a knife.

Poor Pinocchio ran immediately to the hearth, where there
was a pot boiling, and he went to uncover it so that he could see
what was inside. But the pot was painted on the wall. Imagine
how he felt. His nose, which was already long, grew at least four
inches longer.

At that point he began to run around the room, rummaging in
all the drawers and in all the cupboards in search of a bit of bread,
even a bit of dry bread, a mere crust, a bone the dog had dis-
carded, a bit of moldy polenta, a fish bone, a cherry pit: in short,
something to chew on. But he found nothing, one big nothing,
absolutely nothing.

And in the meantime his hunger was growing, and it kept on
growing, and poor Pinocchio's only relief came from yawning; he

yawned so wide and long that a few times his mouth stretched all the way to his ears. And after he yawned, he would spit, and it felt like he was spitting his stomach out.

And then, crying and despairing, he said:

"The Talking Cricket was right. I was wrong to rebel against my father and run away from home . . . If my father were here, I wouldn't be yawning to death now! Oh, what an awful disease hunger is!"

Then suddenly he thought he saw something round and white on top of the garbage heap, something that resembled a hen's egg. In less than a flash he took a leap and tackled it. It really was an egg.

It's impossible to describe the puppet's joy; you'll have to be able to imagine it. Almost believing it was a dream, he turned the egg over and over again in his hands, touching it and kissing it, and as he kissed it he said:

"And now how shall I cook it? I'll make an omelet out of it! . . . No, better to cook it on a griddle! . . . Or perhaps it would be tastier if I fried it in a skillet? Or if I soft-boiled it? No, the quickest way of all is to cook it in a griddle or in a pan; I'm too eager to eat it!"

No sooner said than done. He put the pan on top of a brazier full of hot embers; he put a little water in the frying pan, instead of oil or butter; and when the water started steaming, crack! . . . He broke the egg open and prepared to drop it into the pan.

But instead of the white and the yolk, out jumped a perfectly cheerful and polite little chick who bowed low and said:

"Thanks a million, Mister Pinocchio, for having saved me the effort of breaking the shell! Good-bye, stay well, and best regards to everyone at home."

Having said this, he spread his wings, slipped out the window, which was open, and flew off out of sight.

The poor puppet stood there as if enchanted, his eyes staring, his mouth hanging open, and the pieces of eggshell in his hand. But when he had recovered from his initial bewilderment, he began to cry, shriek, and stamp his feet on the ground in despair, and as he was crying he said:

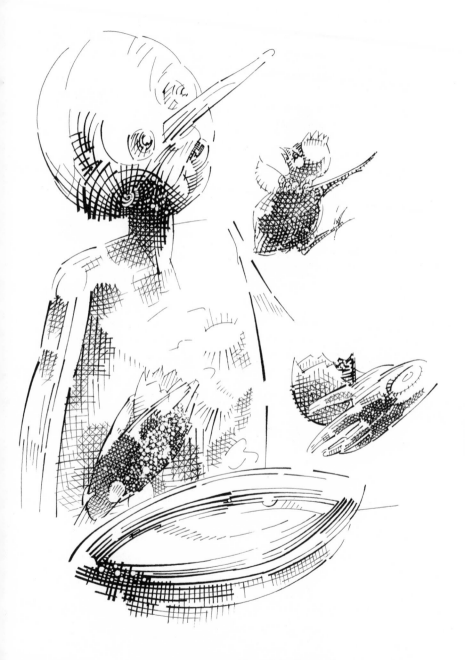

"Mille grazie, signor Pinocchio, d'avermi
risparmiata la fatica di rompere il guscio!"

"The Talking Cricket was right after all! If I hadn't run away from home and if my father were here I wouldn't be dying of hunger now! Oh, what an awful disease hunger is! . . ."

And since his stomach continued to rumble more loudly than ever and he didn't know what to do to quiet it down, he decided to go out and take a quick visit to the nearby village, where he hoped to find some charitable person who might give him a bit of bread.

CHAPTER SIX

Pinocchio falls asleep with his feet on the brazier, and the next morning he wakes up with his feet completely burned off.

*I*T JUST HAPPENED to be a horrible, hellish night. Thunder crashed, flashes of lightning seemed to set the sky on fire, and a terribly cold and bitter wind whistled angrily and raised an immense cloud of dust that made all of the trees in the countryside creak and hiss.

Pinocchio was awfully afraid of thunder and lightning; it was just that his hunger was stronger than his fear. And it was for this reason that he opened the front door and set off at full speed. After a hundred or so leaps he arrived at the village, panting and with his tongue hanging out like a hunting dog.

But he found everything dark and deserted. The shops were closed, the doors to the houses closed, the windows closed, and there wasn't even a dog in the street. It looked like the land of the dead.

Then Pinocchio, in the throes of desperation and hunger, latched on to the doorbell of a house and began to ring it without pause, saying to himself:

"Someone will look out."

In fact, a little old man with a nightcap on his head did look out, and he shouted quite crossly:

"Fatti sotto e para il cappello."

"What do you want at this hour?"

"Would you do me a favor, and give me a little bread?"

"Wait right there, and I'll be back in a minute," answered the little old man, thinking he was dealing with one of those wild young toughs who amuse themselves at night by ringing doorbells just to harass respectable people who are sleeping peacefully.

After half a minute the window opened again, and the voice of the same little old man shouted to Pinocchio:

"Come closer and hold out your hat."

Pinocchio took off his pathetic little hat, but as he went to hold it out he felt an enormous bucketful of water rain down on him, which drenched him from head to toe as if he were a pot of dried-up geraniums.

He went home wet as a chick, nearly finished off by exhaustion and hunger. And since he no longer had the strength to stand up on his feet, he sat down, resting his soaked and mud-splashed feet on a brazier full of hot embers.

And there he fell asleep; and as he was sleeping his wooden feet caught fire and burned down very slowly, until they became ashes.

And Pinocchio continued to sleep and to snore, as if his feet belonged to someone else. Finally at daybreak he woke up, because someone had knocked at the door.

"Who is it?" he asked, yawning and rubbing his eyes.

"It's me!" answered a voice.

The voice was Geppetto's.

E lì si addormentò; e nel dormire, i piedi . . .
adagio adagio . . . diventarono cenere.

CHAPTER SEVEN

**Geppetto returns home and gives
the puppet the breakfast the poor
man had brought for himself.**

*P*OOR PINOCCHIO, whose eyes were still filled with sleep, hadn't yet realized that his feet had burned off, so that as soon as he heard his father's voice, he sprang off the stool with the intention of running to unbolt the door. But instead, after staggering along for two or three steps, he fell flat on the floor.

And when he hit the ground he made the same sound that a sack of wooden soup ladles would have made falling from the fifth floor.

Meanwhile, Geppetto was shouting "Open up!" from the street.

"My dear father, I can't," answered the puppet, crying and rolling around on the ground.

"Why can't you?"

"Because they've eaten my feet."

"And who has eaten them?"

"The cat," said Pinocchio, looking at the cat, which was amusing itself by batting around some wood shavings with its front paws.

"Open up, I'm telling you!" repeated Geppetto, "or else when I get inside, I'll give you the cat, I will!"

"I can't stand up straight, you've got to believe me. Oh, poor me! Poor me; I'll have to walk on my knees for the rest of my life!"

Believing that all this whining was more of the puppet's mischief, Geppetto decided once and for all to put an end to it, and after climbing up the wall, he entered the house through the window.

At first he intended to say and do who knows what; but then, when he saw his Pinocchio stretched out on the ground, and truly missing his feet, he felt a wave of tenderness come over him, and after he had gathered him up in his arms, he started kissing him and caressing and cuddling him a thousand times over. And with large tears streaming down his cheeks, he said to Pinocchio, sobbing:

"My dear little Pinocchio! How is it that you burned your feet?"

"I don't know, Father, but believe me, it's been a hellish night and I'll remember it as long as I live. There was thunder and lightning and I was very hungry, and then the Talking Cricket said to me: 'It serves you right: you've been a bad boy, and you deserve it,' and I said to him: 'You watch out, Cricket!' and he said to me: 'You're a puppet and you've got a wooden head,' and I threw the handle of a hammer at him, and he died, but it was his fault because I didn't mean to kill him, and the proof is that I put a little frying pan on the hot embers in the brazier, but the chick jumped out and said: 'Good-bye . . . and best regards to everyone at home.' And my hunger was growing even stronger, which is why that little old man with the nightcap looked out the window and said to me: 'Come closer and hold out your hat,' and with that bucketful of water on my head — since asking for a little bread is nothing to be ashamed of, is it? — I came right back home, and seeing as I was still very hungry I put my feet up on the brazier to get dry, and you came back, and I ended up with them burned off, and in any case I'm still very hungry and I don't have my feet anymore! Boo hoo! . . . Boo hoo! . . . Boo hoo hoo!"

And poor Pinocchio started to cry and scream so loudly that they could hear him from three miles away.

Geppetto, who had only understood one thing in that whole muddled account, namely that the puppet felt like he was dying of hunger, took three pears out of his pocket, and holding them out to him, he said:

"These three pears were supposed to be for my breakfast, but I'll be glad to give them to you. Eat them, and may they do you good."

"If you want me to eat them, do me the favor of peeling them."

"Peeling them?" answered Geppetto, amazed. "I would never have thought, my dear boy, that you were so picky and such a finicky eater. That's bad! In this world, from the time you're a child, you need to get used to tasting anything and eating everything, because you never know how things may turn out for you. Anything can happen! . . ."

"You're probably right," interrupted Pinocchio, "but I'll never eat a piece of fruit unless it's peeled. I can't stand peels."

And that good man Geppetto pulled out a little knife and, armed with saintly patience, he peeled the three pears and put all the peels on one corner of the table.

After Pinocchio had eaten the first pear in two mouthfuls, he started to throw away the core; but Geppetto caught hold of his arm and said to him:

"Don't throw it away; in this world anything may come in handy."

"But I truly don't intend to eat the core!" shouted the puppet, throwing himself from side to side like a snake.

"Who knows? Anything can happen," repeated Geppetto, remaining calm.

The fact of the matter is that instead of being thrown out the window, the three cores were placed on the corner of the table, in the company of the peels.

After Pinocchio had eaten, or more precisely devoured, the three pears, he gave a very long yawn and whined:

"I'm still hungry!"

"But my dear boy, I have nothing left to give you."

"Nothing, nothing at all?"

"I casi son tanti!"

"All I have are these pear peels and cores."

"Oh well!" said Pinocchio, "if there's nothing else, I'll eat a peel."

And he started chewing. At first he twisted up his mouth a little; but then in the wink of an eye he gobbled down all the peels, one after the other, and after the peels the cores, too. And when he had finished eating every last thing, he patted his stomach contentedly and said, quite pleased with himself:

"Now I sure feel good!"

"So you see," observed Geppetto, "that I was right when I told you that you shouldn't make a habit out of having either too discriminating or too delicate a palate. My dear boy, you never know how things may turn out for you in this world. Anything can happen! . . ."

CHAPTER EIGHT

**Geppetto makes new feet for Pinocchio and
sells his own coat to buy him a spelling book.**

*A*s soon as he had gotten rid of his hunger, the puppet immediately started grumbling and crying, because he wanted a new pair of feet.

But to punish him for his mischief, Geppetto let him cry and despair for half a day. Then he said to him:

"And why should I make you new feet? Just to see you run away from home again?"

"I promise you," said the puppet, sobbing, "that starting from today I'll be a good boy . . ."

"All children say that," replied Geppetto, "when they want something."

"I promise you that I'll go to school, I'll study, and I'll distinguish myself . . ."

"All children repeat that same story when they want something."

"But I'm not like other children! I'm better than all of them, and I always tell the truth. I promise you, Father, that I'll learn a trade and that I'll be the consolation and the staff of your old age."

Even if Geppetto put on a tyrant's face, his eyes were full of tears and his heart swollen with compassion when he saw his poor Pinocchio in that sorrowful state. So he gave not another word in reply, but took hold of his tools and two small pieces of seasoned wood, and set to work with the utmost care.

And in less than an hour the feet were done: two nimble little feet, lean and sinewy, that looked like they had been carved by a master artist.

Then Geppetto said to the puppet:

"Close your eyes and go to sleep!"

And Pinocchio closed his eyes and pretended to sleep. And while he was pretending to be asleep, Geppetto stuck the two feet in place with a little glue that he had dissolved in an eggshell. And he did such a good job of sticking them on that you couldn't even see where they were attached.

As soon as the puppet realized he had feet, he jumped down off the table where he had been lying and started doing a thousand little leaps and capers, as if he had gone crazy with great happiness.

"To repay you for everything you've done for me," said Pinocchio to his father, "I want to go to school right away."

"That's a good boy."

"But I'm going to need some clothes to go to school."

So Geppetto, who was poor and didn't have even a cent in his pocket, made him a simple little suit of flowered paper, a pair of shoes of tree bark, and a little cap of bread crumbs.

Pinocchio immediately ran to look at himself in a basin full of water, and he was so happy with what he saw that he said, as he strutted to and fro:

"I certainly do look like a gentleman!"

"And so you do," replied Geppetto, "because, and always keep this in mind, it's not nice clothes that make a gentleman, but rather clean clothes."

"By the way," added the puppet, "I'm still missing something that I'll need for school: indeed, the most important and necessary thing of all."

"And what's that?"

"I'm missing a spelling book."

"You're right, but how do you get one?"

"That's easy enough: you go to a bookstore and you buy one."

"And what about money?"

"I don't have any."

"Nor do I," added the good old man, becoming sad.

And although he was quite a lighthearted boy, Pinocchio became sad, too; because poverty, when it's real poverty, can be understood by everyone, even children.

"Never mind!" cried out Geppetto all of a sudden, standing up. And when he had slipped on his old moleskin jacket, all full of patches and darning, he left the house at a run.

After a short time he returned; and when he returned, he had a spelling book for his son in his hand, but he no longer had his jacket. The poor man was in his shirtsleeves, and it was snowing outside.

"What happened to your jacket, Father?"

"I sold it."

"Why did you sell it?"

"Because I was too hot in it."

Pinocchio grasped the meaning of this answer at once, and as he was unable to rein in the emotion that surged from his good heart, he flung his arms around Geppetto's neck and started to kiss him all over his face.

"E la casacca, babbo?"

CHAPTER NINE

**Pinocchio sells his spelling book so that
he can go and see the puppet theater.**

*W*HEN IT HAD STOPPED snowing Pinocchio, with his
fine new spelling book under his arm, set off down the
road that led to the school, and as he was walking his little brain
dreamed up a thousand thoughts and built a thousand castles in
the air, each more lovely than the next.

And as he was talking to himself, he said:

"Today at school I want to learn to read immediately, then tomorrow I'll learn to write, and the day after tomorrow I'll learn arithmetic. Then I'll earn lots of money with my skills, and with the first
money that I have in my pocket I want to immediately buy my father
a lovely wool jacket. But what am I saying, wool? I'll get him one
that's all silver and gold, with diamond buttons. And the poor man
sure deserves it, since after all, if he's in shirtsleeves now it's because
he wanted to buy me books and educate me . . . and in this freezing
weather! No one but fathers are capable of certain sacrifices!"

As he was saying this he was very moved, but then he seemed
to hear, in the distance, the sound of fifes and the beating of a bass
drum: *pi-pi-pi, pi-pi-pi, boom boom boom boom.*

He stopped and listened carefully. The sounds were coming
from the end of a very long crossroad that led to a little village
built by the sea.

"Bravo bue!"

"I wonder what that music is? It's too bad I have to go to school; otherwise . . ."

And he stood there, confused. In any case, he needed to come to a decision: either he went to school or he went to hear the fifes.

"Today I'll go hear the fifes, and tomorrow to school; there's always time to go to school," that rascal finally said, shrugging his shoulders.

No sooner said than done. He turned down the crossroad and raced off, kicking up his heels. The more he ran, the more distinctly he heard the sound of the fifes and the thuds of the bass drum: *pi-pi-pi, pi-pi-pi, pi-pi-pi, boom boom boom boom.*

And then suddenly he found himself in the middle of a square all full of people crowded around a large tent that was made of wood and canvas and painted a thousand different colors.

"What's that tent?" asked Pinocchio, turning to a little boy who was from the village.

"Read the poster and you'll find out; it's written right there."

"I'd be happy to read it, but it just so happens that I don't know how to read today."

"A fine ox you are! Then I'll read it to you. For your information, what's written on that poster in letters as red as fire is: GRAND PUPPET THEATER."

"Did the show start long ago?"

"It's starting now."

"And how much does it cost to get in?"

"Four pennies."

Pinocchio, who was burning with the fever of curiosity, lost all reserve and said, without the least shame, to the little boy with whom he was speaking:

"Would you give me four pennies until tomorrow?"

"I'd be happy to give them to you," answered the other boy, mocking him, "but it just so happens that I can't give them to you today."

"I'll sell you my jacket for four pennies," the puppet said to him then.

"What would I do with a jacket made of flowered paper? If it gets rained on, there's no way of getting it off."

"Do you want to buy my shoes?"

"All they're good for is lighting a fire."

"How much will you give me for my cap?"

"That would really be a fine purchase! A cap made of bread crumbs! The mice would probably come and eat it off my head!"

Pinocchio was on tenterhooks. He was just about to make a final offer, but he didn't have the courage; he hesitated, he wavered, he suffered. Finally he said:

"Will you give me four pennies for this new spelling book?"

"I'm a child, and I don't buy things from other children," answered his little interlocutor, who was more sensible than he was.

"I'll take the spelling book for four pennies," shouted a ragseller who had been present during the conversation.

And the book was sold right there on the spot. And to think that poor Geppetto was at home shivering with cold in his shirtsleeves, because he had bought the spelling book for his son!

CHAPTER TEN

The puppets recognize their brother Pinocchio
and give him a grand welcome, but just as they're
doing this the puppet master Fire-Eater comes out,
and Pinocchio runs the risk of coming to a bad end.

*W*HEN PINOCCHIO entered the marionette theater something happened that nearly caused a revolution.

You should know that the curtain was up and the show had already begun.

On the stage you could see Harlequin and Punch bickering with one another, and, as usual, they were threatening to exchange a charge of smacks and wallops at any moment.

The very attentive audience was nearly dying of laughter as it listened to the squabbling between the two puppets, who were gesticulating and insulting each other in every way possible and so realistically that they might have been two rational creatures, two people of this world.

Suddenly, out of the blue, Harlequin stops acting and, turning toward the audience and pointing to someone at the back of the orchestra section, begins to cry out dramatically:

"Celestial deities! Do I dream or wake? And yet, that *is* Pinocchio down there!"

"It really is Pinocchio!" shouts Punch.

"It's truly him!" shrieks Madam Rosaura, peeking out from the back of the stage.

"It's Pinocchio! It's Pinocchio!" all the puppets cry out in

... in mezzo a tantro arruffio ...

chorus, jumping out from the wings. "It's Pinocchio! It's our brother Pinocchio! Long live Pinocchio!"

"Pinocchio, come up here to me!" shouts Harlequin, "come and throw yourself into the arms of your wooden brothers!"

At this affectionate invitation, Pinocchio takes a flying leap, and from the back of the orchestra ends up in the front section; then he jumps again, and from the front section lands on the orchestra conductor's head, and from there he darts up onto the stage.

It's impossible to imagine the hugs, the neck squeezing, the friendly pinches, and the knocks on the head given in recognition of true and sincere brotherhood that, in the midst of all the commotion, Pinocchio received from the actors and actresses of that dramatico-vegetal company.

This spectacle was moving, it goes without saying; but when the members of the audience saw that the show had come to a halt, they grew impatient and started to yell:

"We want the show. We want the show!"

It was all wasted breath, since instead of carrying on with the performance the puppets doubled the racket and their shouting, and after they had hoisted Pinocchio onto their shoulders, they paraded him in triumph before the footlights.

At that point the puppet master came out. He was a huge man who was so ugly that the mere sight of him was enough to give you a fright. He had a nasty old beard that was as black as an inkblot and so long that it reached from his chin down to the ground; suffice it to say that with each step he took he trampled on it. His mouth was as wide as an oven, his eyes looked like two lanterns of red glass with a flame burning inside, and his hands cracked a large whip made of snakes and foxtails twisted together.

At the unexpected appearance of the puppet master, everyone was struck dumb, and no one dared even to take a breath. You could have heard a fly. Those poor puppets, male and female, were shaking like leaves on a tree.

"Why have you come and created all this confusion in my theater?" the puppet master asked Pinocchio, with the deep voice of an ogre with a terrible head cold.

"Please believe me, most illustrious Sir; it wasn't my fault! . . ."

"That's enough! We'll settle our score this evening."

In fact, after the performance was over, the puppet master went into the kitchen, where a fine mutton he had prepared for his dinner was slowly turning on the spit. And since he didn't have enough wood to finish roasting and browning it, he called Harlequin and Punch and said to them:

"Bring me the puppet you'll find hanging on the nail over there. It appears to be a puppet made of very dry wood, and I'm sure that when I throw it on the fire it will give me a lovely flame for my roast."

At first Harlequin and Punch hesitated. But then, since they were frightened by the terrible look their master gave them, they obeyed, and after a little while they returned to the kitchen carrying poor Pinocchio, who, wriggling like an eel out of water, shrieked desperately:

"My dear father, save me! I don't want to die, no, I don't want to die!"

"Babbo mio, salvatemi! Non voglio morire, no, non voglio morire!"

CHAPTER ELEVEN

**Fire-Eater sneezes and pardons Pinocchio,
who then saves his friend Harlequin from death.**

J CAN'T DENY THAT the puppet master Fire-Eater (for this was his name) looked to be a frightful man, especially with that awful black beard of his that covered his whole chest and all of his legs like an apron, but deep down he wasn't a bad man. And the proof was that when he saw poor Pinocchio being brought before him, thrashing about every which way and yelling "I don't want to die, I don't want to die!" he was immediately touched and began to feel sorry for him. And after resisting for a good while, he could no longer stand it, and let out a resounding sneeze.

At that sneeze Harlequin, who up until then had been as despondent and downcast as a weeping willow, put on a cheerful face and, leaning toward Pinocchio, whispered to him under his breath:

"Good news, brother! The puppet master has sneezed, and that's a sign that he feels sorry for you, so at this point you're safe."

Now you should know that whereas all other men either cry or at least pretend to dry their eyes when they feel pity for someone, Fire-Eater, had, instead, the bad habit of sneezing every time he was really moved. It was just a different way of letting other people know that he had a sensitive heart.

After he had sneezed, the puppet master kept up his gruff manner and shouted at Pinocchio:

"Stop crying! Your wailing has given me a funny feeling in the bottom of my stomach . . . I feel a pang that's almost, that's almost . . . Atchoo! Atchoo!" and he sneezed two more times.

"Bless you!" said Pinocchio.

"Thank you. And are your father and mother still alive?" Fire-Eater asked him.

"My father is; I never knew my mother."

"Who knows how sad your old father would be if I had you thrown onto those burning coals now! Poor old man! I sympathize with him! . . . Atchoo, atchoo, atchoo," and he sneezed three more times.

"Bless you!" said Pinocchio.

"Thank you! On the other hand, I'm to be sympathized with, too, since as you can see, I don't have enough firewood to finish roasting my piece of mutton, and to be truthful, in this case you would have come in very handy. But by now I'm feeling pity for you, so never mind. Instead of you I'll take one of the puppets from my company to burn under the spit. Hey there, gendarmes!"

At this command, two wooden gendarmes immediately appeared. They were quite tall, very thin, wore three-cornered hats on their heads, and carried unsheathed sabers in their hands.

The puppet master said to them in a wheezy voice:

"Go get me that Harlequin over there, tie him up tightly, and then throw him on the fire to burn. I want my mutton to be well roasted!"

Imagine poor Harlequin! His fright was so great that his legs folded under him, and he fell flat on the floor.

At the sight of that heartrending spectacle, Pinocchio went and threw himself down at the puppet master's feet, and as he wept his eyes out and watered every hair of the puppet master's terribly long beard with his tears, he began to say in a pleading voice:

"Have pity, Sir Fire-Eater!"

"There are no sirs here!" the puppet master harshly replied.

"Olà, giandarmi!"

"Have pity, Sir Knight!"

"There are no knights here!"

"Have pity, Sir Commendatore!"

"There are no commendatores here!"

"Have pity, Excellency!"

When he heard himself called Excellency, the puppet master immediately pursed his lips, and, suddenly becoming more human and reasonable, he said to Pinocchio:

"All right then, what do you want from me?"

"I beg you to grant poor Harlequin a pardon!"

"There's no granting pardons here. If I spare you, then I've got to put him on the fire, because I want my mutton to be well roasted."

"In that case," cried Pinocchio courageously, getting up and throwing off his cap of bread crumbs, "in that case I know what my duty is. Come forward, gendarmes! Tie me up and throw me in those flames over there. No, it's not right that poor Harlequin, my true friend, should have to die for me!"

These words, pronounced in a loud voice and with heroic diction, made all the puppets who witnessed the scene cry. The gendarmes themselves, although they were made of wood, wept like two little suckling lambs.

At first Fire-Eater remained hard-hearted and as immovable as a piece of ice, but then, little by little, he too started to soften up, and to sneeze. And after he had sneezed four or five times, he opened his arms affectionately and said to Pinocchio:

"You're one terrific boy! Come over here and give me a kiss."

Pinocchio ran right over and, scrambling up the puppet master's beard like a squirrel, went and planted a lovely kiss on the tip of his nose.

"So is the pardon granted?" asked poor Harlequin in a wispy voice that could barely be heard.

"The pardon is granted!" answered Fire-Eater. Then he added, sighing and shaking his head:

"Oh well! For this evening I'll resign myself to eating my

mutton half-raw; but too bad for whoever happens to be around next time!"

At the news that the pardon had been granted, all the puppets ran up onto the stage, and after they had lit the lamps and chandeliers as if for a gala performance, they began to jump around and dance. Dawn came and they were still dancing.

CHAPTER TWELVE

**The puppet master Fire-Eater gives Pinocchio a
present of five gold coins to take to his father,
Geppetto, but instead Pinocchio lets himself be duped
by the Fox and the Cat and goes off with them.**

THE NEXT DAY Fire-Eater called Pinocchio aside and asked him:

"What's your father's name?"

"Geppetto."

"And what's his trade?"

"Being a poor man."

"Does he earn a lot?"

"He earns just enough never to have a cent in his pocket. Imagine that he had to sell the only jacket he owned to buy me a spelling book for school. A jacket that had so many patches and darns that it looked like an open wound."

"Poor devil! I almost feel sorry for him. Here are five gold coins. Go and take them to him immediately, and send him my best regards."

As can easily be imagined, Pinocchio thanked the puppet master a thousand times. He hugged all the puppets of the company one by one, even the gendarmes, and then, beside himself with happiness, he set off, intending to return home.

But he hadn't yet gone a quarter of a mile down the road when

"Povero diavolo!"

he encountered a Fox who was lame in one foot and a Cat who was blind in both eyes. They were making their way along, each helping the other like good companions in misfortune. The Fox, who was lame, leaned on the Cat as he walked; and the Cat, who was blind, let himself be guided by the Fox.

"Good day, Pinocchio," said the Fox, greeting him politely.

"How is it that you know my name?" asked the puppet.

"I know your father well."

"Where have you seen him?"

"I saw him yesterday on his doorstep."

"And what was he doing?"

"He was in his shirtsleeves, and he was shivering with cold."

"Poor Father! But, God willing, from today on he'll shiver no more!"

"Why is that?"

"Because I've become a grand gentleman."

"You, a grand gentleman?" said the Fox, and he started to laugh in a vulgar, mocking manner. And the Cat laughed too, but he combed his whiskers with his front paws so that you couldn't see it.

"There's very little to laugh about," yelled Pinocchio, in a huff. "I'm truly sorry to make your mouths water, but these, if you understand anything about it, are five beautiful gold coins."

And he pulled out the coins that Fire-Eater had given him.

At the pleasant sound of those coins the Fox, with an involuntary movement, extended the leg that appeared to be crippled, and the Cat opened both of his eyes so wide that they looked like two green lanterns; but then he closed them again immediately, and, in fact, Pinocchio didn't notice a thing.

"And now," the Fox asked him, "what do you want to do with those coins there?"

"First of all," answered the puppet, "I want to buy my father a fine new jacket made of silver and gold, with diamond buttons, and then I want to buy a spelling book for myself."

"For yourself?"

"C'è poco da ridere."

"That's right, because I want to go to school and start studying seriously."

"Look at me!" said the Fox. "Because of my silly passion for study I lost a leg."

"Look at me!" said the Cat. "Because of my silly passion for study I lost the sight in both of my eyes."

Just then a white Blackbird, who was perched on a hedge at the side of the road, gave his usual call and said:

"Pinocchio, don't listen to the advice of bad companions, or else you'll be sorry!"

Poor Blackbird, he should never have said that! The Cat took a big leap and pounced on him and without even giving him the time to say *oh!* ate him up in one bite, feathers and all.

When he had finished eating and had wiped his mouth, the

Cat closed his eyes again and began once more to pretend that he was blind, just like before.

"Poor Blackbird!" said Pinocchio to the Cat. "Why did you treat him so badly?"

"I did it to teach him a lesson. That way, the next time he'll learn not to stick his beak into other people's conversations."

They had gotten more than halfway there when the Fox, stopping unexpectedly, said to the puppet:

"Do you want to double your gold coins?"

"What do you mean?"

"Do you want to make your five miserable gold pieces become a hundred, a thousand, two thousand?"

"I wish! But how?"

"How? It's very easy. Instead of going on home, you'd have to come with us."

"And where do you intend to take me?"

"To the Land of the Featherbrains."

Pinocchio thought about it for a bit and then said firmly:

"No, I don't want to come. I'm close to home now, and I want to return home, where my father is waiting for me. Who knows how much the poor old man suffered yesterday when he saw that I wasn't coming back. I'm afraid I've been a bad son, and the Talking Cricket was right when he said, 'Disobedient children can't come to any good in this world.' And I've learned that at my own expense, since I've come up against so many misfortunes, and last night at Fire-Eater's house, too, I was in danger of . . . Brrr! I'm getting goose bumps just thinking about it!"

"So," said the Fox, "you really want to go home? Well, go ahead then, and so much the worse for you."

"So much the worse for you!" repeated the Cat.

"Think it over carefully, Pinocchio, because you're kicking fortune in the pants."

"Fortune in the pants!" repeated the Cat.

"Between today and tomorrow your five gold pieces would have become two thousand."

"Two thousand!" repeated the Cat.

"But however is it possible for them to become so many?" asked Pinocchio, his mouth hanging open in amazement.

"I'll explain it to you right now," said the Fox. "You should know that in the Land of the Featherbrains there's a blessed field, which everyone calls the Field of Miracles. You make a little hole in this field and you put a gold piece, for example, in it. Then you cover up the hole with a bit of earth, you water it with two pails of fountain water, you sprinkle a pinch of salt over it, and in the evening you go calmly to bed. In the meantime, during the night the gold piece germinates and blossoms, and the next morning as soon as you get up you go back to the field, and what do you find? You find a lovely tree full of as many gold pieces as a fine stalk of wheat has grains in the month of June."

"So then," said Pinocchio, growing more and more astonished, "if I buried my five gold pieces in that field, how many would I find there the next morning?"

"That's quite easy to calculate," answered the Fox. "You can do it on your fingers. Suppose each gold piece yields a cluster of five hundred pieces. Multiply five hundred by five, and the next morning you'll find two thousand five hundred brand-new gold pieces jangling in your pocket."

"Oh, how lovely!" shouted Pinocchio, dancing with joy. "As soon as I pick these gold pieces, I'll keep two thousand for myself and I'll give the two of you the other five hundred as a present."

"A present for us?" shouted the Fox, growing indignant and acting insulted. "God forbid!"

"Forbid!" repeated the Cat.

"We," the Fox went on, "do not work out of vile self-interest; we work exclusively for the purpose of making others rich."

"Others rich!" repeated the Cat.

"What good people!" thought Pinocchio to himself; and suddenly forgetting about his father, the new jacket, the spelling book, and all the fine resolutions he had made, he said to the Fox and the Cat:

"Let's go right away; I'm coming with you."

CHAPTER THIRTEEN

The Red Lobster Inn.

*O*N AND ON and on they walked, and finally, as evening was falling, they reached the Red Lobster Inn, dead tired.

"Let's stop here for a while," said the Fox. "Just long enough to get a bite to eat and to rest a few hours. At midnight we'll start out again, so that tomorrow at dawn we can be at the Field of Miracles."

After they had gone into the tavern, all three of them sat down at a table, although none of them had any appetite.

The poor Cat, who was feeling seriously sick to his stomach, was able to eat nothing more than thirty-five red mullets in tomato sauce and four portions of tripe Parmesan. And since the tripe didn't seem to have enough seasoning for him, he made up for it by asking three times for more butter and grated cheese!

The Fox would have gladly nibbled at something, too, but since the doctor had ordered him to follow a very strict diet he had to be content with a simple hare in sweet-and-sour sauce, accompanied by a very light side dish of plump spring chickens and young cockerels. After the hare, he ordered, to tease his appetite, a little casserole of grouse, partridge, rabbit, frog, lizard, and paradise raisins, and after that he wanted nothing else. He felt such nausea at the sight of food, he said, that he couldn't bring anything to his lips.

The one who ate the least of all was Pinocchio. He asked for a

Aveva tanta nausea per il cibo, diceva lei,
che non poteva accostarsi nulla alla bocca.

slice of walnut and a crust of bread, and he left everything on his plate. With the obsessive thought of the Field of Miracles in his head, the poor boy had gotten an advance case of indigestion from gold coins.

After they had finished their dinner, the Fox said to the host:

"Give me two good rooms, one for Mister Pinocchio and the other for me and my companion. Before we leave we'll be taking a little snooze. But remember that we want to be awakened at midnight so that we can get on with our journey."

"Yessirs," answered the host, and gave the Fox and the Cat a wink, as if to say: "I get the drift; it's a deal!"

As soon as Pinocchio got into bed he fell right to sleep and started dreaming. And in his dream he saw himself in the middle of a field, and this field was crowded with little trees full of clusters, and these clusters were full of gold pieces that, as they swung in the wind, went clink, clink, clink, almost as if they were trying to say "whoever wants us, come and get us." But just when Pinocchio was at the best part, when, that is, he stretched out his hand to grab handfuls of those lovely coins and put them in his pocket, he was suddenly awakened by three violent blows on the door of his room.

It was the host coming to tell him that midnight had struck.

"And are my companions ready?" the puppet asked him.

"They certainly are ready! They left two hours ago."

"Why in such a big hurry?"

"The Cat got word that his eldest kitten, who's suffering from frostbite of the paws, was in danger of dying."

"And did they pay for the dinner?"

"You've got to be kidding! Those two are too well bred to slight your lordship like that."

"Too bad! It would have been a great pleasure to receive such a slight!" said Pinocchio, scratching his head. Then he asked:

"And where did these good friends of mine say they would wait for me?"

"At the Field of Miracles, tomorrow morning at the break of dawn."

Pinocchio paid a gold piece for his dinner and those of his companions, and then set off.

You could actually say that he groped his way off, for outside the tavern it was dark, so very dark that you couldn't see from here to there. You couldn't hear a leaf move in the surrounding countryside. There were only a few awful night birds who, every now and then, banged their wings on Pinocchio's nose as they crossed the road from one hedge to the other. When this happened Pinocchio would jump backward in fright and shout: "Who goes there?" and the echo off the surrounding hills would repeat from afar: "Who goes there? Who goes there? Who goes there?"

In the meantime, as he was walking he noticed, on a tree trunk, a tiny little animal that was glowing with a pale and opaque light, like a small candle in a transparent porcelain lamp.

"Who are you?" Pinocchio asked.

"I am the shade of the Talking Cricket," answered the little animal in a barely audible voice that seemed to come from the world beyond.

"What do you want with me?" said the puppet.

"I want to give you some advice. Go back and take the four gold pieces that are left to your poor father, who has been crying and despairing since he lost sight of you."

"Tomorrow my father will become a grand gentleman, for these four gold pieces will turn into two thousand."

"Don't trust people who promise to make you rich between morning and night, my boy. They're usually either madmen or swindlers! Listen to me: go back."

"But I, on the other hand, want to go on."

"The hour is late! . . ."

"I want to go on."

"The night is dark . . ."

"I want to go on."

"The road is dangerous . . ."

"I want to go on."

"Remember that children who are naughty and want to do things their own way sooner or later regret it."

"The same old story. Good night, Cricket."

"Good night, Pinocchio, and may the heavens save you from dampness and assassins."

As soon as he had said these last words, the Talking Cricket suddenly went out, like a candle goes out when you blow on it, and the road was left darker than before.

CHAPTER FOURTEEN

**Because he didn't listen to the good
advice of the Talking Cricket,
Pinocchio runs into the assassins.**

EALLY," THE PUPPET said to himself as he started off on his journey once again, "how unlucky we poor children are! Everyone yells at us, everyone warns us, everyone gives us advice. If they had their way, they would all get it into their minds to become our fathers and our teachers, every last one of them, even the Talking Crickets. There you have it: because I didn't want to listen to that annoying Cricket, who knows how many misfortunes I'm supposed to be in for, according to him! I'm even supposed to meet up with assassins! It's a good thing that I don't believe in assassins, nor have I ever believed in them. In my opinion, assassins were invented on purpose by fathers, to frighten children who want to go out at night. And even if I did run into them here on the road, you think they would frighten me? Not a chance. I'd go right up to them and shout: 'Mister Assassins, what do you want with me? Remember that I'm not one to fool around with! So you can leave now and go about your business, and not a word more!' If I really did speak to those poor assassins like that they would flee like the wind, I can just see them now. And if they were so bad-mannered that they refused to run away, then I would run away, and I'd put an end to it that way . . ."

But Pinocchio wasn't able to finish this argument, because at that moment he seemed to hear a very faint rustling of leaves behind him.

He turned around to look, and in the dark he saw two dreadful black figures, completely wrapped in two coal sacks, who were running leaping toward him, on their tiptoes, as if they were two ghosts.

"Here they are, for real!" he said to himself, and not knowing where to hide the four gold pieces, he hid them in his mouth: to be more precise, under his tongue.

Then he tried to run away. But he hadn't yet taken the first step when he felt himself grabbed by the arms and heard two horrible, cavernous voices that said:

"Your money or your life!"

Pinocchio couldn't answer with words, on account of the coins that he had in his mouth, and so he bowed and scraped a thousand times and mimed a thousand different gestures to make it clear to those two hooded figures — of whom all you could see were their eyes, through the holes in the sacks — that he was a poor puppet and that he didn't even have a false penny in his pocket.

"Come on, come on! Less chitchat, and out with the money!" the two bandits shouted threateningly.

And the puppet signaled with his head and hands, as if to say: "I don't have any."

"Get your money out or you're dead," said the taller of the assassins.

"Dead!" repeated the other.

"And after we've killed you, we'll kill your father, too!"

"Your father, too!"

"No, no, no, not my poor father!" shouted Pinocchio in a desperate voice; but when he shouted like that, you could hear the gold pieces in his mouth.

"Ah, you scoundrel! So you've got your money hidden under your tongue? Spit it out right now!"

But Pinocchio was tough!

"Ah! You're playing deaf? Just you wait, we'll get you to spit it out!"

In fact, one of them grabbed the puppet by the tip of his nose, and the other one took hold of him by his protruding chin, and then they started to pull him roughly, one this way and the other that way, so that he would be forced to open his mouth. But to no avail. It seemed as if the puppet's mouth had been nailed and riveted shut.

Then the shorter assassin pulled out a nasty-looking knife and tried to wedge it like a lever or a chisel between the puppet's lips; but Pinocchio, as quick as lightning, sank his teeth into the assassin's hand, and after he had bitten it clean off spit it out. And imagine his astonishment when he realized that, instead of a hand, he had spit a cat's paw onto the ground.

Encouraged by this first victory, he freed himself by force from the assassins' claws, leaped over the hedge at the side of the road, and began to flee through the countryside. And the assassins ran after him like two dogs after a hare; and the one who had lost a paw ran on just one leg, and it's never been discovered how he did it.

After running ten miles Pinocchio could go on no longer. Realizing that he was done for, he climbed up the trunk of a very tall pine tree and sat himself down among the uppermost branches. The assassins tried to climb up, too, but when they were halfway up the trunk they slipped and fell back down to the ground, skinning their hands and feet.

Nonetheless, they didn't give up. On the contrary: after they had arranged a bundle of dry kindling at the foot of the pine tree, they set it on fire. In less than no time the pine tree caught on fire and began to blaze like a candle in the wind. Seeing that the flames were climbing higher and higher and not wanting to end up like a roasted pigeon, Pinocchio took a huge leap from the top of the tree, and away he ran again through the fields and vineyards. And the assassins ran after him, still ran after him, never getting tired.

In the meantime daylight began to glimmer and they were still

. . . raccolto un fastello di legna secche a
piè del pino, vi appiccarono il fuoco.

chasing after one another, when all of a sudden Pinocchio found his way blocked by a wide and very deep ditch, full to the top with dirty, stagnant water that was the color of coffee with milk. What to do? "One, two, three!" shouted the puppet, and after he took a good running start, he jumped over to the other side. And the assassins jumped, too, but since they hadn't calculated the distance right, plop! . . . they fell right into the ditch. When Pinocchio heard the thud and the splash of the water, he yelled, laughing and continuing to run:

"Have a nice bath, Mister Assassins!"

And he was already imagining them good and drowned when he turned around to look and realized instead that they were both running after him, still wrapped in their sacks, with water streaming off them as if they were two leaky baskets.

CHAPTER FIFTEEN

**The assassins chase after Pinocchio
and after catching up with him hang
him from a branch of the Great Oak.**

*A*T THIS POINT the puppet had lost heart and was just
about to throw himself on the ground and give up when,
casting his eyes around, he saw a little snow-white house glowing
palely in the distance against the dark green of the trees.

"If I had enough breath to get to that house, maybe I'd be
safe!" he said to himself.

And without waiting another minute he started off again, running through the forest at full speed. And the assassins still ran
after him.

After a desperate race of almost two hours he finally arrived,
gasping for breath, at the door of that little house, and he
knocked.

No one answered.

He knocked again, more loudly this time, because he heard
the sound of his persecutors' footsteps and their heavy and labored breathing growing closer. The same silence. .

When it became clear to him that knocking served no purpose, out of desperation he began to kick the door and bang his
head against it. And then a lovely Little Girl appeared at the
window. She had blue hair and a face as white as a waxen image;

her eyes were closed and her hands were crossed on her chest, and without the slightest movement of her lips she said, in a faint voice that seemed to come from the world beyond:

"There is no one in this house. They are all dead."

"Well, then, you open up for me!" shouted Pinocchio, crying and pleading with her.

"I am dead, too."

"Dead? But then what are you doing up there at the window?"

"I am waiting to be taken away in a casket."

As soon as she had said this, the Little Girl disappeared, and the window closed again without making a sound.

"Oh lovely Little Girl with the blue hair," shouted Pinocchio, "open up, for goodness' sake. Have pity on a poor boy who's being chased by assass —"

But he wasn't able to finish the word, because he felt himself being grabbed by the neck, and the same two awful voices rumbled threateningly:

"You won't get away from us now!"

When the puppet saw death flash before his eyes, he got such a bad case of the shakes that, as he was shaking, the joints of his wooden legs and the four gold pieces hidden under his tongue started chattering.

"Well then?" the assassins asked him, "are you going to open that mouth of yours or not? Ah! You're not answering? . . . Never mind, this time we'll make you open it!"

And after they had taken out two terribly long, awful-looking knives that were as sharp as razor blades, *zap!* and then *zap!* . . . they dealt him two blows in the middle of his back.

But luckily for him, the puppet was made out of very hard wood, and for this reason the blades shattered into a thousand slivers and the assassins were left looking into each other's faces with only knife handles in their hands.

"I see," one of them said then, "we've got to hang him! Let's hang him!"

"Hang him!" repeated the other.

Intanto s'era levato un vento impetuoso di tramontana . . .

No sooner said than done. They tied his hands behind his back, and after they had passed a slipknot over his neck, they left him hanging on a branch of a large tree called the Great Oak.

Then they sat down there on the grass and waited for the puppet to give his last kick, but after three hours the puppet still had his eyes open, his mouth closed, and was kicking harder than ever.

When they had finally grown bored of waiting, they turned to Pinocchio and said to him, sneering:

"Good-bye until tomorrow. When we come back tomorrow, let's hope that you'll be polite enough to allow yourself to be found good and dead, with your mouth hanging open."

And they left.

In the meantime a blustery north wind had risen, and, blowing and howling furiously, it slammed the poor hanging puppet from side to side, making him swing as violently as the clapper of a bell ringing at full peal. And that swinging caused him to have the most acute spasms, and the slipknot, which grew tighter and tighter around his neck, was choking him.

Little by little his eyes misted over, and although he felt death approaching, he nevertheless still hoped that at any moment some merciful soul might show up to help him. But as he continued to wait and saw that no one was coming, no one at all, his poor father came to mind again . . . and he stuttered, on the verge of dying:

"Oh, my dear father! If only you were here! . . ."

And he didn't have the breath to say anything more. He closed his eyes, opened his mouth, stretched out his legs, and, after giving a great shudder, hung there as if he were frozen stiff.

CHAPTER SIXTEEN

**The lovely Little Girl with the blue hair
has the puppet taken down; she puts him
to bed and summons three doctors to
determine whether he is dead or alive.**

*J*UST AS POOR Pinocchio, who had been hung by the assassins on a branch of the Great Oak, was starting to appear more dead than alive, the lovely Little Girl with the blue hair looked out the window again. Moved to pity by the sight of that miserable soul who, suspended by his neck, was whirling to the rhythm of the gusts of the north wind, she clapped her hands together three times and then gave three small taps.

At this signal a loud sound of wings beating with impetuous urgency was heard, and a large Falcon landed on the windowsill.

"What is your command, my gracious Fairy?" said the Falcon, lowering his beak in reverence (because you should know that the Little Girl with the blue hair was actually none other than a wonderfully good Fairy who had lived in the vicinity of that forest for more than a thousand years).

"Do you see that puppet hanging on a branch of the Great Oak?"

"I see him."

"Well, then: fly down there immediately, use your strong beak to break the knot that is keeping him suspended in the air, and lay him delicately on the grass at the foot of the oak."

The Falcon flew away and after two minutes returned, saying: "I have done what you have ordered me to do."

"And how did you find him? Dead or alive?"

"Looking at him, he appeared to be dead, but he must not be properly dead yet, because as soon as I loosened the slipknot that was squeezing his neck, he let out a sigh, and murmured in a low voice: 'Now I feel better! . . .' "

Then the Fairy clapped her hands together and gave two small taps, and there appeared a magnificent Poodle who walked upright on his hind legs, exactly as if he were a man.

The Poodle was dressed like a coachman in formal uniform. He wore a small three-cornered hat decorated with gold braid, a white wig covered with curls that hung down to his neck, a chocolate-colored jacket with diamond buttons and two large pockets to hold the bones that his mistress gave him at dinner, a pair of crimson velvet breeches, silk stockings, elegant pumps, and on his back a sort of umbrella sheath made of blue satin, to hold his tail when the weather turned to rain.

"Come now, be a good boy, Medoro!" said the Fairy to the Poodle. "Go and have the finest coach in my carriage house harnessed, and then take the forest road. When you reach the Great Oak, you'll find a poor half-dead puppet lying on the grass underneath. Pick him up gently, lay him carefully on the cushions in the coach, and bring him to me here. Do you understand?"

To show that he had understood, the Poodle wagged the blue satin sheath on his back three or four times and took off like a racehorse.

After a little while, out of the carriage house emerged a lovely little coach that was the color of air, all padded with canary feathers and lined on the inside with whipped cream and filled ladyfingers. The little coach was drawn by a hundred pairs of white mice, and the Poodle, who was in the box, cracked his whip to the right and to the left, like a driver afraid of being late.

A quarter of an hour had not yet gone by when the carriage returned, and the Fairy, who was waiting at the doorstep, took the poor puppet in her arms, and when she had brought him to a

La carrozzina era tirata da cento pariglie di topini bianchi . . .

little room with walls of mother-of-pearl, she immediately had the most famous doctors of the area summoned.

The doctors arrived immediately, one after the other: that is, there arrived a Raven, an Owl, and a Talking Cricket.

"I would like to know from you gentlemen," said the Fairy, turning to the three doctors gathered around Pinocchio's bed, "I would like to know from you gentlemen whether this hapless puppet is dead or alive!"

At this invitation, the Raven was the first to come forward. He felt Pinocchio's pulse, then he felt his nose, then the little toes of each foot; and when he had felt everything thoroughly, he solemnly pronounced these words:

"It is my belief that the puppet is already dead; but if by some stroke of bad luck he were not dead, then it would be a sure indication that he is still alive!"

"Vorrei sapere da lor signori se questo
disgraziato burattino sia vivo o morto!"

"I am sorry," said the Owl, "to have to contradict the Raven, my illustrious friend and colleague. In my opinion, on the contrary, the puppet is still alive; but if by some stroke of bad luck he were not live, then it would be a sign that he is truly dead."

"And aren't you going to say anything?" the Fairy asked the Talking Cricket.

"I say that the best thing a prudent doctor can do when he doesn't know what he's talking about is to keep quiet. Besides, that puppet's face is not new to me; I've known him for some time!"

Pinocchio, who until then had been as motionless as a real piece of wood, gave a sort of convulsive shudder that made the whole bed shake.

"That puppet there," the Talking Cricket went on, "is a consummate scoundrel . . ."

Pinocchio opened his eyes and then shut them again immediately.

"He's a lousy rascal, a lazybones, a bum . . ."

Pinocchio hid his face under the sheets.

"That puppet there is a disobedient son who is going to make his poor father die of heartbreak!"

At this point a stifled sound of weeping and sobbing was heard in the room. Imagine everyone's surprise when they lifted the sheets a little and realized that the one weeping and sobbing was Pinocchio.

"When the dead weep, it is a sign that they are on the road to recovery," the Raven solemnly said.

"It pains me to contradict my illustrious friend and colleague," added the Owl, "but in my opinion, when the dead cry, it is a sign that they are sorry to be dying."

CHAPTER SEVENTEEN

Pinocchio eats sugar but doesn't want to take his medicine, although when he sees the gravediggers coming to take him away he finally does take it. Then he tells a lie and as a punishment his nose grows.

*A*S SOON AS THE three doctors left the room the Fairy drew close to Pinocchio and, after touching his forehead, realized that he was running a remarkably high fever.

Then she dissolved a certain fine white powder in half a glass of water, and as she held it out to the puppet, she said to him lovingly:

"Drink it, and in a few days you'll be all better."

Pinocchio looked at the glass, screwed up his mouth, and then asked in a whiny voice:

"Is it sweet or bitter?"

"It's bitter, but it's good for you."

"If it's bitter I don't want it."

"Listen to me: drink it."

"I don't like bitter things."

"Drink it, and when you've drunk it, I'll give you a lump of sugar to take the bad taste away."

"Where is the lump of sugar?"

"It's right here," said the Fairy, taking it out of a gold sugar bowl.

"First I want the lump of sugar, and then I'll drink that terrible bitter water . . ."

"Do you promise?"

"Yes . . ."

The Fairy gave him the lump of sugar, and after crunching it up and swallowing it in barely a second Pinocchio licked his lips and said:

"Wouldn't it be nice if sugar were medicine, too! . . . I'd take the cure every day."

"Now keep your promise and drink these few little drops of water, which will give you back your health."

Pinocchio reluctantly took the glass in his hand and poked the tip of his nose into it; then he brought the glass to his mouth; then he poked the tip of his nose into it again; finally he said:

"It's too bitter! Too bitter! I can't drink it."

"How can you say that if you haven't even tasted it?"

"I can imagine it! I can tell from the smell. First I want another lump of sugar . . . and then I'll drink it!"

So the Fairy, with all the patience of a good mother, put another bit of sugar in his mouth, and then presented him again with the glass.

"I can't drink it like this!" said the puppet, making a thousand faces.

"Why not?"

"Because that pillow down there on my feet is bothering me."

The Fairy took away the pillow.

"It's no use! I can't drink it like this either."

"What else is bothering you?"

"The bedroom door that's half open is bothering me."

The Fairy went over and closed the bedroom door.

"When it comes down to it," cried out Pinocchio, bursting into tears, "I don't want to drink this horrible, bitter water, no, no, no!"

"You'll be sorry, my boy . . ."

"I don't care . . ."

"You've got a serious illness . . ."

"I don't care . . ."

"Your fever will carry you off to the world beyond in a few hours . . ."

"I don't care . . ."

"Aren't you afraid of death?"

"Not at all afraid! . . . It's better to die than to drink that awful medicine."

At this point, the bedroom door opened wide, and in came four rabbits, black as ink, carrying a little casket on their shoulders.

"What do you want with me?" shouted Pinocchio, sitting up in bed, terrified.

"We have come to get you," answered the biggest rabbit.

"To get me? . . . But I'm not dead yet!"

"Not yet; but you have only a few more minutes to live, since you have refused to drink the medicine that would have cured you of your fever!"

"Oh, my dear Fairy, oh, my dear Fairy!" the puppet started to shriek, "give me that glass right away . . . Hurry up, for goodness' sake, because I don't want to die, no . . . I don't want to die."

And taking the glass with both hands, he emptied it in a flash.

"Oh, well!" said the rabbits. "This time we made the trip for nothing." And, pulling the little casket back onto their shoulders, they left the room grumbling and muttering under their breath.

The fact of the matter is that just a few minutes later Pinocchio jumped down off the bed, all better; because, you should know, wooden puppets have the privilege of rarely falling ill and of getting better very quickly.

And the Fairy, when she saw him running and romping around the room, as lively and cheerful as a cockerel singing his first song, said to him:

"So my medicine really did do you some good?"

"Better than good! It brought me back to this world!"

"And so how come you had to be begged so hard to drink it?"

"It's just that we children are all like that! We're more afraid of medicine than of being sick."

"Shame on you! Children should know that a good medication taken in time can save them from serious illnesses and perhaps even from death . . ."

"Oh! The next time, though, I won't make you beg me so much! I'll remember those black rabbits, with the casket on their shoulders . . . and then I'll take the glass right in my hand, and I'll drink it right down!"

"Now come over here to me a minute and tell me how it happened that you found yourself in the hands of the assassins."

"It went like this: the puppet master Fire-Eater gave me five gold coins and said: 'Here, bring these to your father!' but instead on the way I met up with a Fox and a Cat, two very respectable people, who said to me: 'Do you want those coins to become a thousand, or two thousand? Come with us, and we'll take you to the Field of Miracles.' And I said: 'Let's go'; and they said: 'Let's stop here at the Red Lobster Inn, and we'll set out again after midnight.' And when I woke up, they weren't there anymore, because they had already left. So I started to walk, and it was night and impossibly dark, and so on the way I ran into two assassins inside two coal sacks, who said to me: 'Get out your money'; and I said: 'I don't have any,' since I had hidden the gold coins in my mouth, and one of the assassins tried to put his hands in my mouth, and I bit his hand off and then spit it out, but instead of a hand I spit out a cat's paw. And the assassins ran after me, and I was racing as fast as I could to get away from them, until they caught up with me, and they hung me by my neck on a tree in this forest and told me: 'Tomorrow we're coming back here, and by then you'll be dead and your mouth will be hanging open, so we'll be able to take the gold coins you're hiding under your tongue from you.'"

"And now where have you put the four coins?" the Fairy asked him.

"I've lost them!" answered Pinocchio, but he was telling a lie, because he actually had them in his pocket.

As soon as he told the lie his nose, which was already long, immediately grew two inches longer.

"And where did you lose them?"

"In the forest nearby."

At this second lie, his nose continued to grow.

"If you lost them in the forest nearby," said the Fairy, "we'll look for them and we'll find them, because everything that you lose in the nearby forest, you always find again."

"Ah! Now that I remember better," replied the puppet, making a mess of things, "I didn't lose the four coins, but without realizing it I swallowed them while I was drinking your medicine."

At this third lie, his nose grew so extraordinarily long that poor Pinocchio could no longer move in any direction. If he turned this way, he hit his nose on the bed or on the windowpanes; if he turned that way, he hit it against the walls or the bedroom door; if he lifted his head a little, he ran the risk of driving it into one of the Fairy's eyes.

And the Fairy looked at him and laughed.

"Why are you laughing?" the puppet asked her, quite confused and worried about that nose of his, which was growing before his very eyes.

"I'm laughing at the lie you told."

"However do you know that I told a lie?"

"Lies, my dear boy, are easily recognized, because there are of two types: there are lies that have short legs, and lies that have a long nose. Yours, as a matter of fact, is one of those with a long nose."

Pinocchio was so ashamed that he didn't know where to hide himself, and so he tried to run out of the room. But he wasn't able to. His nose had grown so much that it could no longer fit through the door.

"... vi sono le bugie che hanno le gambe corte, e le bugie
che hanno il naso lungo: la tua per l'appunto ..."

CHAPTER EIGHTEEN

**Pinocchio meets up with the Fox and the
Cat again and goes with them to plant the
four coins in the Field of Miracles.**

*A*s you can imagine, the Fairy let the puppet cry and
scream for a good half hour over that nose of his that
could no longer fit through the bedroom door; and she did this to
teach him a harsh lesson and so that he would correct himself of
the bad habit of telling lies, the worst habit that a child can have.
But when she saw him transformed that way, with his eyes pop-
ping out of his head in great despair, she was moved to pity and
clapped her hands together, and at that signal in through the bedroom window came a thousand large birds called woodpeckers,
who all landed on Pinocchio's nose and started to peck at it so
hard, so very hard, that in a few minutes that enormous and ex-
cessive nose was reduced to its natural size.

"How good you are, my dear Fairy," said the puppet, drying his
eyes. "And how much I love you!"

"I love you, too," the Fairy answered, "and if you want to stay
with me, you will be my little brother and I will be your good little
sister."

"I'd gladly stay . . . but what about my poor father?"

"I've thought of everything. Your father has already been in-
formed, and before night falls he'll be here."

"Really?" shouted Pinocchio, jumping with joy. "In that case, my dear little Fairy, if it's all right with you, I'd like to go and meet him! I can't wait to be able to kiss that poor old man who has suffered so much for me!"

"Go, if you like, but be careful not to lose your way. Take the road through the forest, and I'm sure you'll run into him."

Pinocchio left, and as soon as he entered the forest he began to run like a deer. But when he had gotten to a certain point, nearly in front of the Great Oak, he stopped, because he seemed to hear people in the undergrowth. In fact, guess who he saw come out onto the road? The Fox and the Cat; that is, the two traveling companions with whom he had dined at the Red Lobster Inn.

"Here's our dear Pinocchio!" shouted the Fox, hugging and kissing him. "How come you're here?"

"How come you're here?" repeated the Cat.

"It's a long story," said the puppet, "and I'll tell you about it when it's more convenient. You should know, though, that the other night when you left me alone at the inn, I met up with the assassins on the road . . ."

"The assassins? . . . Oh, you poor friend of mine! And what did they want?"

"They wanted to steal the gold coins."

"Abominable!" said the Fox.

"Abominable!" repeated the Cat.

"But I began to escape," went on the puppet, "and they kept on running after me, until they caught up with me and hanged me from a branch of that oak tree . . ."

And Pinocchio indicated the Great Oak, which was just a few steps away.

"Have you ever heard anything worse?" said the Fox. "What a world we're condemned to live in! Where will men of honor like us find a safe refuge?"

As they were talking in this manner, Pinocchio noticed that the Cat was limping on his right front leg, because at the end of it the whole paw, including the claws, was missing. And so he asked:

"What did you do to your paw?"

The Cat wanted to give an answer, but he became confused. So the Fox immediately said:

"My friend is too modest, and that's the reason he's not answering. I'll answer for him. You should know, then, that an hour ago we met an old wolf on the road who was faint with hunger and begged us for some charity. Since we didn't even have a fish bone to give him, what did my friend, who truly has a heart the size of Caesar's, do? He bit a paw off one of his front legs and threw it to that poor animal so that he could satisfy his hunger."

And as he was saying this the Fox dried a tear.

Pinocchio, who was also moved, went over to the Cat and whispered in his ear:

"If all cats were like you, how lucky mice would be!"

"And now what are you doing in these parts?" the Fox asked the puppet.

"I'm waiting for my father, who should be getting here any minute."

"And your gold coins?"

"I still have them in my pocket, all except one, which I spent at the Red Lobster Inn."

"And to think that instead of four coins, by tomorrow they could become a thousand, even two thousand! Why don't you listen to my advice? Why don't you go and plant them in the Field of Miracles?"

"Today that's impossible; I'll go another day."

"Another day and it will be too late!" said the Fox.

"Why?"

"Because that field has been bought by a great nobleman, and from tomorrow on no one will be allowed to plant money there anymore."

"How far from here is the Field of Miracles?"

"Just over a mile. Do you want to come with us? In half an hour you'll be there. You plant your four coins right away; after a few minutes you pick two thousand of them; and this evening you return here with your pockets full. Do you want to come with us?"

Pinocchio hesitated a little before answering, because the good Fairy, old Geppetto, and the warnings from the Talking Cricket came back to mind. But then he ended up doing what all children without a shred of good sense and without a heart do: that is, he ended up giving a little shake of his head, and then he said to the Fox and the Cat:

"Let's go, then; I'm coming with you."

And they set out.

After walking for half a day they came to a city called Saptrap. As soon as he entered the city, Pinocchio saw that all the streets were populated by mangy dogs yawning with hunger, sheared sheep shivering with cold, hens without crests or wattles begging for a kernel of corn, large butterflies that could no longer fly because they had sold their beautiful colored wings, tailless peacocks that were ashamed to let themselves be seen, and pheasants who hopped around quietly, mourning their glittering feathers of silver and gold, by now lost for good.

In the midst of this crowd of beggars and shamefaced paupers, every now and then an elegant carriage would pass by with either a Fox or a thieving Magpie or some ghastly bird of prey inside.

"So where's the Field of Miracles?" asked Pinocchio.

"It's just a few steps away."

No sooner said than done: they crossed the city, and when they were outside the city walls they stopped in a secluded field that looked pretty much like any other field.

"Here we are," said the Fox to the puppet. "Now get down on the ground, dig a little hole in the field with your hands, and put the gold coins in it."

Pinocchio obeyed him. He dug the hole, placed the remaining four gold coins in it, and then covered up the hole again with some dirt.

"Now, then," said the Fox, "go to the nearby ditch, get a pailful of water, and water the soil where you planted the coins."

Pinocchio went to the ditch, and since he didn't have a pail

Dopo aver camminato una mezza giornata arrivarono a
una città che aveva nome "Acchiappa-citrulli."

with him right then he took off one of his shoes, and after he had filled it with water, he watered the dirt covering the hole. Then he asked:

"Is there anything else to do?"

"Nothing else," answered the Fox. "Now we can leave. But you come back in about twenty minutes, and you'll find a little tree already sprouting from the ground, its branches full of coins."

The poor puppet, beside himself with great joy, thanked the Fox and the Cat a thousand times and promised to give them a wonderful gift.

"We don't want gifts," answered those two devils. "We're satisfied with having taught you the way to get rich without working for it, and we're as happy as larks about that."

That said, they bid Pinocchio good-bye and, wishing him a good harvest, went off about their own business.

CHAPTER NINETEEN

**Pinocchio is robbed of his gold coins, and
as punishment he gets four months in prison.**

W HEN THE PUPPET had gotten back to the city, he
started to count the minutes, one by one, and when he
thought it was time he hurried back to the road that led to the
Field of Miracles.

And as he walked along at a hurried pace, his heart was
beating hard, and going tick-tock, tick-tock, like a grandfather
clock when it's running at full speed. And in the meantime he
was thinking to himself:

"And what if instead of a thousand coins, I found two thousand
of them on the branches of that tree? . . . And if instead of two
thousand, I found five thousand? And if instead of five thousand,
I found a hundred thousand? Oh, what a fine gentleman I would
become, then! . . . I'd have a beautiful palace, a thousand little
wooden horses and a thousand stables to play with, a cellar full of
rosolio and *alkermes* liqueurs, and a library brimming with can-
died fruit, cakes, panettone, almond brittle, and wafers spread
with whipped cream."

Daydreaming in this manner, he arrived in the vicinity of the
field, and there he stopped to see if by chance he could catch
sight of a tree with its branches full of coins; but he saw nothing.
He took another hundred steps forward: nothing; he went into the

field: nothing . . . he went right over to the little hole where he had buried his gold pieces: nothing. At that point he became worried, and, forgetting the rules of etiquette and good manners, he took one of his hands out of his pocket and gave himself a very long scratch on the head.

Just then he heard a loud shriek of laughter ring in his ears, and, looking up, he saw a large Parrot perched in a tree, delousing the few feathers that he still had on him.

"Why are you laughing?" Pinocchio asked in an irritated voice.

"I'm laughing because as I was picking my lice off I tickled myself under my wings."

The puppet didn't answer. He went to the ditch, and after he had filled the same old shoe with water he began to water the dirt covering the gold coins again.

All of a sudden another shriek of laughter, even more impertinent than the first, was heard in the silent solitude of that field.

"That's it!" shouted Pinocchio, getting angry, "might one know, bad-mannered Parrot, what you're laughing at?"

"I'm laughing at those Featherbrains who believe every sort of foolishness and who fall into the traps of those who are more clever than they are."

"Are you perhaps talking about me?"

"Yes, I'm talking about you, poor Pinocchio; you who are so lacking in common sense that you believe that money can be planted and reaped in fields, just like beans and pumpkins. I believed that once, too, and today I'm still paying the price for it. Now (but it's too late!) I've had to persuade myself that if you want to put together a little money honestly you have to know how to earn it, either by the work of your own hands or with the brains in your own head."

"I don't understand you," said the puppet, already starting to tremble with fear.

"Never mind! I'll explain myself more clearly," continued the Parrot. "You should know, then, that while you were in town, the

Fox and the Cat returned to this field. They took the gold coins you had buried, and then they raced off like the wind. Whoever catches up with them now is a fine runner indeed!"

Pinocchio stood there with his mouth open, and since he didn't want to believe the Parrot's words, with his hands and his fingernails he began to dig up the soil that he had watered. He dug and dug and dug and made a hole so deep that a haystack could have stood upright in it, but the coins were no longer there.

Overcome by despair at this point, he raced back to town and went directly to the judge in the courthouse to report the two crooks that had robbed him.

The judge was an ape of the gorilla family, an old ape who was worthy of respect on account of his advanced age, his white beard, and especially the gold-rimmed glasses without lenses that he was obliged to wear all the time due to an eye infection from which he had suffered for many years.

In the presence of the judge, Pinocchio related the iniquitous fraud of which he had been a victim, leaving out nothing; he gave the first name, last name, and descriptions of the crooks, and in conclusion, he asked for justice.

The judge listened to him with great kindness; he became most intensely involved in the tale; he was touched, he was moved; and when the puppet had nothing left to say, he extended his hand and rang a bell.

At that loud ring there appeared two bulldogs dressed as gendarmes.

Then the judge, indicating Pinocchio to the gendarmes, said to them:

"That poor devil was robbed of four gold coins, so take him away and put him in prison immediately."

When the puppet heard himself being given this sentence completely out of the blue, he stood there dumbfounded and wanted to protest. But the gendarmes, to avoid any useless waste of time, covered his mouth and took him off to the pen.

And there he had to stay for four months — four interminable

"Quel povero diavolo è stato derubato . . . pigliatelo
dunque, e mettetelo subito in prigione."

months — and he would have stayed even longer if something very lucky had not happened to come about. Because you should know that the young Emperor who ruled over the city of Saptrap, having carried off a triumphant victory over his enemies, ordered grand public festivities, light shows, fireworks, horse and veloci-pede races, and, as the greatest sign of exultation, he even ordered that the jails be opened and all the crooks set free.

"If the others are getting out of prison, I want to get out, too," said Pinocchio to the jailer.

"Not you," said the jailer, "because you're not among those who qualify."

"I beg your pardon," replied Pinocchio, "I'm a crook, too."

"In that case you're absolutely right," said the jailer, and taking off his cap respectfully and bidding him farewell, he opened the prison doors and let him escape.

CHAPTER TWENTY

**Freed from prison, he sets out to return
to the Fairy's house, but along the way
he encounters a horrible serpent
and then gets caught in a trap.**

*I*MAGINE PINOCCHIO'S happiness when he found himself free. Without further ado, he immediately left the city and got back on the road that should have led him back to the Fairy's little cottage.

On account of the drizzly weather, the road had become one big mud puddle where you sank in up to your knees. But the puppet paid no heed. Tortured by the desire to see his father and his little sister with the blue hair again, he ran along, bounding forward like a greyhound, and as he ran he got splashed by mud all the way up to his cap. All the while he was saying to himself: "So many terrible things have happened to me . . . And I deserve them all, because I'm a headstrong and peevish puppet! . . . And I always want to do things my way, without listening to those who love me and who have a thousand times more common sense than I do! . . . But from this time on I resolve to change my life and become a well-behaved and obedient boy . . . Besides, by now I've already seen that children, when they're disobedient, always end up on the losing end and nothing ever works out right for them. And do you think my father has waited for me? . . . Will I find him at the Fairy's house? It's been so long since I've seen the poor man that I'm just dying to caress him a thousand times over and finish him off with kisses! And will the Fairy forgive me for the terrible thing I did to her? . . . And to think of all the attention and all the loving care that I've received from her . . . and to think that if I'm still alive today, I owe it to her! . . . But can there be a more ungrateful and heartless boy than me? "

As he was saying this, he suddenly stopped, frightened, and took four steps backward.

What had he seen?

He had seen a large Serpent stretched out across the road. It had green skin, fiery eyes, and a pointed tail that smoked like a chimney.

It's impossible to imagine the puppet's fear. When he had retreated more than a quarter of a mile, he sat down on a little pile of stones and waited for the Serpent to go off on his own business once and for all and leave the road free.

He waited one hour, two hours, three hours; but the Serpent was still there, and even from a distance you could see the red glow of his fiery eyes and the column of smoke that was rising up from of the tip of his tail.

Then Pinocchio, pretending to be courageous, drew to within a few steps of the Serpent and in a sweet, ingratiating, and faint little voice said to him:

"Excuse me, Mister Serpent, but would you do me the favor of moving yourself a little to one side, just enough to let me get by?"

It was like talking to a wall. No one moved.

Then he began again in the same little voice:

"You should know, Mister Serpent, that I'm going home, where my father is waiting for me, and that I haven't seen him for such a long time! . . . So would it bother you if I continued on my way?"

He waited for some sign of an answer to that question, but the answer didn't come. On the contrary, the Serpent, who until then had appeared to be sprightly and full of life, became immobile and almost stiff. His eyes closed and his tail stopped smoking.

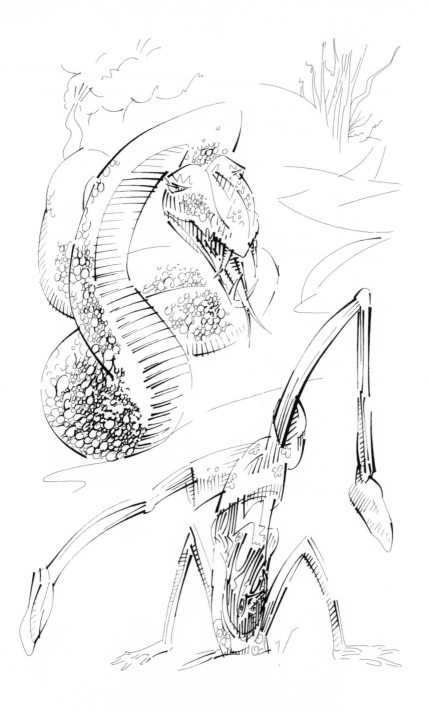

. . . che sgambettava a capo fitto con una velocità
incredibile, il Serpente . . . ridi, ridi, ridi, alla fine . . .

"Could he really be dead?" said Pinocchio, rubbing his hands together with great joy; and without letting a minute go by, he went to step over him, so that he could get to the other side of the road. But he hadn't yet finished lifting his leg when the Serpent suddenly shot up like a spring, and as the puppet was pulling away, frightened, he tripped and fell to the ground.

Indeed, he took such a bad fall that he ended up on the road with his head stuck in the mud and his feet straight up in the air.

At the sight of that upside-down puppet kicking his feet in the air at an incredible speed, the Serpent was seized by such a fit of laughter that he laughed and laughed and laughed until finally he burst a vein in his chest from the strain of laughing too much; and that time he really did die.

Then Pinocchio started running again, so that he would arrive at the Fairy's house before it got dark. But along the way, no longer able to resist his terrible hunger pangs, he jumped into a field with the intention of picking a few bunches of muscatel grapes. He should never had done that!

As soon as he got to the grapevine, *crack!* . . . he felt his feet clamped between two sharp irons, which made him see all the stars in the sky.

The poor puppet had fallen into a trap set there by some farmers to nab some large martens that were the scourge of all the chicken coops in the neighborhood.

CHAPTER TWENTY-ONE

**Pinocchio is caught by a farmer who forces
him to be the watchdog for his chicken coop.**

*A*s YOU CAN IMAGINE, Pinocchio began to cry, shriek,
and beg for mercy; but his cries and shouts were of no
use, since there wasn't a house in sight anywhere nearby and
there wasn't a living soul that passed by on the road.

Meanwhile, night fell.

In part because of the pain of the trap that was cutting into his
shins, in part because of his fear at finding himself alone and in
the dark in the middle of those fields, the puppet was almost
about to faint when all of a sudden he saw a firefly go by above his
head, and he called to her, saying:

"Oh little Firefly, would you do me the favor of freeing me
from this agony?"

"Poor boy!" replied the Firefly, stopping to look at him with
pity. "How come you ended up with your legs locked in those
sharp irons?"

"I came into the field to pick two bunches of these muscatel
grapes, and . . ."

"But were the grapes yours?"

"No . . ."

"Then who taught you to take what belongs to others?"

"I was hungry . . ."

"O Lucciolina, mi faresti la carità di liberarmi da questo supplizio?"

"Hunger, my boy, isn't a good reason for taking things that aren't ours . . ."

"That's true, that's true!" shouted Pinocchio, crying, "but I'll never do it again."

At this point the dialogue was interrupted by a very faint sound of footsteps that were getting closer and closer. It was the owner of the field who was tiptoeing over to see if one of the martens that ate his chickens at night had been caught in the trap he had set.

And when he took the lantern out from under his overcoat, he was quite astonished to realize that instead of a marten, there was a boy caught in the trap.

"Ah, you dirty little thief!" said the enraged farmer, "so you're the one who's been stealing my hens!"

"No, not me, not me!" shouted Pinocchio, sobbing. "I just came into the field to get two bunches of grapes!"

"Those who steal grapes are perfectly capable of stealing chickens, too. Just leave it to me; I'll teach you a lesson that you'll remember for a good while."

And he opened the trap, grabbed the puppet by the scruff of his neck, and carried him back home, like you would carry a suckling lamb.

When he got to the barnyard in front of the house, he flung the puppet to the ground and, keeping one foot on his neck, said to him:

"It's late now and I want to go to bed. We'll settle our score tomorrow. Meanwhile, since the dog that kept watch for me at night died today, you'll take his place starting right now. You'll be my watchdog."

No sooner said than done. He slipped a large collar covered with brass spikes onto the puppet's neck and fastened it so tightly that Pinocchio wouldn't be able to take it off by passing his head through it. A long iron chain was attached to the collar, and the chain was fastened to the wall.

"If," said the farmer, "it starts to rain tonight, you can use that wooden shed as a doghouse; the straw that my poor dog used as his bed for four years is still in there. And if by some stroke of bad luck the thieves show up, remember to cock your ears and bark."

After this last bit of advice, the farmer went into the house and locked the door with a huge bolt, and poor Pinocchio was left crouching in the barnyard, more dead than alive on account of the cold and his hunger and fear. And every now and then he angrily thrust his hands under the collar that clamped his throat and said, weeping:

"It serves me right! . . . I'm afraid it serves me right! I insisted on being a lazybones, a bum . . . I insisted on listening to bad companions, and that's why I'm still hounded by misfortune. If I had been a respectable little boy, like so many other boys, if I had had the desire to study and to work, if I had stayed at home with my poor father, I wouldn't find myself here in the middle of these fields being a watchdog at a farmer's house. Oh, if only I could be born again! . . . But it's too late now, I'll just have to be patient!"

After this little outburst, which came straight from his heart, he went into the shed and fell asleep.

CHAPTER TWENTY-TWO

**Pinocchio discovers the thieves, and as
a reward for being faithful he is set free.**

*A*ND HE HAD ALREADY been sleeping soundly for more
than two hours when around midnight he was woken by
the murmuring and whispering of strange little voices that
seemed to be coming from the barnyard. He stuck the tip of his
nose through a hole in the shed and saw four small, dark-coated
animals that looked like cats huddled together in council. But
they weren't cats. They were martens: little carnivorous animals
with a special weakness for eggs and spring chickens. One of these
martens separated herself from her companions, went to the hole
in the shed, and said in a low voice:

"Good evening, Melampo."

"My name's not Melampo," answered the puppet.

"Well who are you, then?"

"I'm Pinocchio."

"And what are you doing in there?"

"I'm the watchdog."

"So where's Melampo? Where's the old dog that used to be in
this shed?"

"He died this morning."

"Died? Poor animal! He was so good! But judging from your
looks, you seem to be a pleasant dog, too."

"I beg your pardon, I'm not a dog!"

"Well, who are you?"

"I'm a puppet."

"And you're the watchdog?"

"Unfortunately, I am; it's my punishment."

"Well then, I propose that we have the same deal that I had with the deceased Melampo; I think you'll be happy with it."

"And what would this deal be?"

"We'll come once a week at night, as we did in the past, to visit the chicken coop, and we'll take away eight hens. Of these hens, we'll eat seven and we'll give one to you, provided — and this must be clear — that you pretend to sleep and never get it in your mind to bark and wake up the farmer."

"And Melampo did just that?"

"He did, and we always got along fine with him. So you can sleep peacefully, and rest assured that before we go off, we'll leave you a chicken, all nice and plucked, on the top of the shed for to-morrow's breakfast. Do we understand each other?"

"Only too well!" answered Pinocchio, and he shook his head in a kind of threatening way, as if he wanted to say: "We'll be discussing this again soon!"

When the four martens felt sure that they had worked things out, they went straight to the chicken coop, which was, as a matter of fact, very close to the doghouse. By the force of their teeth and claws they opened the wooden gate that blocked off the entrance, and then they slinked in, one after the other. But they hadn't even finished going in when they heard the gate slam shut very loudly.

Pinocchio was the one who had shut it and, not content merely to have shut it, he placed a large stone in front of it as a prop, just to be on the safe side.

And then he started to bark; and barking just as if he were a watchdog, he went: "Bow-wow-bow-wow."

At that barking, the farmer jumped out of his bed, got his rifle, and, looking out the window, asked:

"Che c'è di nuovo?"

"What's going on now?"

"The thieves are here!" answered Pinocchio.

"Where are they?"

"In the chicken coop."

"I'll come down right away."

And in fact, faster than you can say "Amen" the farmer came down. He ran into the chicken coop, and after he had caught the four martens and tied them up in a sack, he said to them, his voice ringing with happiness:

"You finally fell right into my hands! I could punish you, but I'm not so vile. Instead, I'll content myself with taking you, to-morrow, to the innkeeper in the nearby town, who will skin you and cook you like a hare in sweet-and-sour sauce. It's an honor that you don't deserve, but generous men like me don't pay atten-tion to such trifles!"

Then he went over to Pinocchio and began to shower him with blandishments; among other things, he asked him:

"How did you manage to discover the plot of these four little thieves? And to think that Melampo, my faithful Melampo, had never noticed a thing!"

At that point the puppet could have told what he knew; he could have told, that is, of the shameful deal that the dog and the martens had made. But remembering that the dog was dead, he immediately thought to himself: "What's the use of accusing the dead? The dead are dead, and the best thing we can do is leave them in peace!"

"When the martens came into the barnyard, were you awake or were you sleeping?" the farmer continued to question him.

"I was sleeping," answered Pinocchio, "but the martens woke me up with their chattering, and one of them came right up to the shed and said to me: 'If you promise not to bark and not to wake up the master, we'll give you a chicken, all nice and plucked!' Did you hear that? To have the nerve to propose such a thing to me! Because you should know that I'm a puppet, and I may have all the flaws in the world, but one I'll never have is telling lies and holding open the bag for dishonest people!"

"Good boy!" shouted the farmer, slapping him on the back. "Those sentiments do you honor, and to prove to you how grateful I am, from this moment you're free to go back home."

And he took the dog collar off him.

CHAPTER TWENTY-THREE

**Pinocchio mourns the death of the lovely
Little Girl with the blue hair. Then he finds
a Pigeon that takes him to the seashore,
where he throws himself into the water
to go to his father Geppetto's aid.**

*A*s soon as Pinocchio no longer felt the terribly heavy
and humiliating weight of that collar around his neck, he
began running away across the fields, and he didn't stop for a
single minute until he had reached the main road that would lead
him to the Fairy's little cottage.

When he got onto the main road, he turned and looked down
onto the plain below, and he saw quite clearly, with his bare eyes,
the forest where he had had the misfortune to encounter the Fox
and the Cat; he saw, rising amid the trees, the top of that Great
Oak from which he had been hanging; but although he looked
this way and that he wasn't able to see the little house belonging
to the lovely Little Girl with the blue hair.

Then he had a sort of sad premonition. With all the strength
left in his legs he broke into a run and a few minutes later found
himself in the meadow where the little white cottage had once
stood. But the little white cottage was no longer there. Instead,
there was a little slab of marble on which one could read these
sorrowful words written in capital letters:

HERE LIES

THE LITTLE GIRL WITH THE BLUE HAIR

WHO DIED OF GRIEF

WHEN SHE WAS ABANDONED BY HER

LITTLE BROTHER, PINOCCHIO

I'll let you imagine how the puppet felt, once he had stumbled through those words. He fell face-down on the ground, and as he was covering the tombstone with a thousand kisses, he burst loudly into tears. He cried all night, and as dawn was breaking the next morning he was still crying, even though his eyes had no more tears; and his wailing and laments were so lacerating and piercing that all the surrounding hills reverberated with their echo.

And as he was crying, he said:

"Oh, my dear little Fairy, why are you dead? . . . Why aren't I dead instead of you, since I'm so bad and you were so good? . . . And where can my father be? Oh, my dear little Fairy, tell me where I can find him, for I want to be with him forever, and never leave him again! Never again! Never again! . . . Oh, my little Fairy, tell me it's not true that you're dead! . . . If you truly love me . . . if you love your little brother, come back to life . . . be alive again, like you were before! . . . Aren't you sorry to see me alone, abandoned by everyone? . . . If the assassins show up, they'll hang me from the branch of that tree again . . . and then I'll die for good. What do you expect me to do in this world, all alone? Now that I've lost you and my father, who'll feed me? Where will I go to sleep at night? Who'll make me a new jacket? Oh! It would be better, a hundred times better, if I died, too! Yes, I want to die! Boo hoo hoo!"

And as he was despairing in this manner, he made as if to tear out his hair; but since his hair was made of wood, he couldn't even have the satisfaction of running his fingers through it.

Meanwhile, a large Pigeon flew by overhead and then hovered in the air with outstretched wings, shouting to him from a great height:

"Tell me, child, what are you doing down there?"

"Don't you see? I'm crying!" said Pinocchio, lifting his head toward that voice and wiping his eyes on the sleeve of his jacket.

"Tell me," resumed the Pigeon, "is there by any chance a puppet by the name of Pinocchio among your friends?"

"Pinocchio? . . . Did you say Pinocchio?" repeated the puppet, immediately jumping to his feet. "I'm Pinocchio!"

At this answer, the Pigeon swooped quickly down and landed on the ground. He was bigger than a turkey.

"Then you must also know Geppetto?" he asked the puppet.

"Of course I know him! He's my poor father! Why, did he talk to you about me? Will you take me to him? Is he still alive, then? For goodness' sake, answer me, is he still alive?"

"I left him three days ago, at the seashore."

"What was he doing?"

"He was building a little boat by himself, so that he could cross the ocean. That poor man has been roaming the world for more than four months in search of you, and since he's never been able to find you, now he's got it into his mind to search for you in the far-off lands of the New World."

"How far is it from here to the seashore?" asked Pinocchio, frantic with worry.

"More than six hundred miles."

"Six hundred miles? Oh, my dear Pigeon, how wonderful it would be if I could have your wings!"

"If you want to come, I'll take you."

"How?"

"Riding on my back. Do you weigh much?"

"Much? Quite the contrary! I'm as light as a leaf."

And right there, without another word, Pinocchio jumped onto the Pigeon's back; and when he had swung one leg over each side, as horseback-riders do, he shouted with great joy: "Gallop, gallop, little horse, for I need to get there soon!"

The Pigeon took off, and in a few minutes he had flown so high that he almost touched the clouds. When they reached that

Il Colombo prese l'aìre e in pochi minuti arrivò col
volo tanto in alto, che toccava quasi le nuvole.

extraordinary height, out of curiosity the puppet turned and looked down, and he was seized by so much fear and such dizziness that to avoid the danger of falling off he twisted his arms ever so tightly around the neck of his feathered mount.

They flew all day. As evening was falling, the Pigeon said:

"I'm very thirsty!"

"And I'm very hungry!" added Pinocchio.

"Let's stop at this dovecote for a few minutes, and then we'll continue our trip, so that tomorrow morning at dawn we'll be at the seashore."

They went into a deserted dovecote, where there was nothing but a basin full of water and a basket overflowing with vetch.

Throughout his whole life the puppet had never been able to stand vetch; to hear him tell it, it gave him nausea, it turned his stomach. But that evening he ate it till he was about to burst, and when he had almost finished, he turned to the Pigeon and said:

"I would never have thought that vetch was so good!"

"You have to persuade yourself, my dear boy," replied the Pigeon, "that when your hunger gets serious and there's nothing else to eat, even vetch becomes exquisite! Hunger is neither too finicky nor too refined!"

After their quick little snack, they set off again on their journey, and away they went! The next morning they arrived at the seashore.

The Pigeon put Pinocchio on the ground and, not even wanting the bother of hearing himself thanked for his good deed, immediately flew off again and disappeared.

The shore was full of people screaming and gesticulating as they looked toward the sea.

"What happened?" Pinocchio asked a little old woman.

"What happened is that a poor father lost his son and decided to get in a little boat and go look for him on the other side of the sea, and the sea is very rough today and the little boat is about to go under . . ."

"Where is the little boat?"

"There it is, down there, right where I'm pointing," said the old woman, indicating a small boat that, when seen at such a distance, looked like a walnut shell with a tiny little man in it.

Pinocchio fixed his eyes in that direction, and after he had looked very carefully, he let out a piercing scream and shouted:

"That's my father! That's my father!"

Meanwhile the little boat, thrown about by the raging waves, would first disappear amid the large breakers, then come back up to the surface. And Pinocchio, who was standing on the top of a cliff, couldn't stop calling his father by name and signaling to him with his hands and with his handkerchief and even with the cap he had on his head.

And although he was very far from the shore, it seemed like Geppetto recognized his son, because he took off his cap, too, and waved it at him, and through his gestures made him understand that he would have gladly come back in; but the sea was so rough that it prevented him from using his oars and from coming in closer to shore.

All of a sudden a terrifying wave broke, and the boat disappeared. Everyone waited for the boat to come back up to the surface, but it could no longer be seen.

"Poor man," said the fishermen who were gathered on the shore, and, muttering a prayer under their breath, they started leaving to go back to their houses.

But just then they heard a desperate scream, and when they turned around they saw a little boy who, from the top of a cliff, was throwing himself into the sea, shouting:

"I want to save my father!"

Since he was all wood, Pinocchio floated easily and swam like a fish. First you would see him disappear underwater, pulled by the force of the waves, then a leg or an arm would reappear, at a great distance from land. They finally lost sight of him and saw him no more.

"Poor boy!" said the fishermen who were gathered on the shore, and, muttering a prayer under their breath, they went back to their houses.

CHAPTER TWENTY-FOUR

Pinocchio arrives at the Island of the Busy Bees and meets up with the Fairy again.

*A*NIMATED BY THE hope of arriving in time to help his poor father, Pinocchio swam the entire night.

And what a horrible night it was! It poured, it hailed, it thundered dreadfully, and the lightning flashed so bright that it looked like it was day.

Toward daybreak he was able to see a long strip of land a short distance away. It was an island in the middle of the sea.

Then he did everything he could to get to that shore, but it was no use. The waves, chasing each other and surging up one after the other, tossed him about as if he were a twig or a piece of straw. Finally, and lucky it was for him, there came a wave so violent and powerful that it hurled him straight onto the sand of the beach.

The blow was of such force that when he hit the ground all of his ribs and joints cracked, but he immediately comforted himself by saying:

"Another narrow escape!"

Meanwhile, little by little the sky cleared up; the sun came out in all of it splendor, and the sea became very calm and as smooth as oil.

Then the puppet spread his clothes out to dry in the sun and started to look this way and that to see if by chance he could make out, on that immense plain of water, a little boat with a tiny man in it. But after looking very carefully, he saw nothing more before him than sky, sea, and the sails of a few ships, but so very far away that they looked like flies.

"If I at least knew what this island is called!" he kept saying. "If I at least knew if this island is inhabited by well-mannered people, I mean by people who don't have the bad habit of hanging children on tree branches! But whoever can I ask? Who, if there's no one here?"

This idea of finding himself alone, alone, alone in the middle of that large uninhabited land, made him so melancholy that he was on the verge of crying when suddenly, at a short distance from the shore, he saw a large fish pass by, going calmly about his own business with his whole head out of the water.

Not knowing what name to call him by, the puppet shouted out loudly, so that he would be heard:

"Hey, Mister Fish, would you allow me to have a word with you?"

"Even two," answered the fish, who was a Dolphin, and so polite that there are only a few of his kind in all the seas of the world.

"Would you do me the favor of telling me if there are any towns on this island where one can eat without running the risk of being eaten?"

"There certainly are," answered the Dolphin. "In fact, you'll find one of them not far from here."

"And which road do you take to get there?"

"You have to take that path over there on the left, and then walk straight, following your nose. You can't miss it."

"Tell me something else. You who are in and about the sea all day and night, you wouldn't by chance have encountered a tiny little boat with my father in it?"

"And who is your father?"

"He is the world's best father, just as I am the worst son that there can be."

"After the storm last night," answered the Dolphin, "the boat has probably gone under."

"And my father?"

"By this time he has probably been eaten up by the terrible Shark, who came to spread destruction and desolation in our waters a few days ago."

"Is this Shark very big?" asked Pinocchio, who was already starting to tremble with fear.

"Is he big!" replied the Dolphin. "To give you an idea of how big, let me tell you that he's bigger than a five-story building, and he has a dreadful mouth that's so wide and deep that a whole railroad train with its engine running could easily pass through it."

"Oh my goodness!" shouted the puppet, frightened; and after he had gotten dressed again in a great hurry he turned to the Dolphin and said:

"Good-bye, Mister Fish; I'm very sorry for any trouble that I've given you, and a thousand thanks for your kindness."

That said, he got right on the path and started walking at a brisk pace: so brisk that it looked almost like he was running. And every time he heard the slightest little noise, he would immediately turn and look behind him, for fear of seeing himself chased by that terrible Shark that was as big as a five-story building and with a railroad train in his mouth.

After he had walked for more than half an hour, he came to a small town called the Town of the Busy Bees. The streets were swarming with people running this way and that about their business. Everyone was working; everyone had something to do. Not one idler or bum was to be found, not even if you searched in every nook and cranny.

"I see," that lazybones Pinocchio said immediately, "this town isn't made for me! I wasn't born to work!"

Meanwhile, he was tormented by hunger, since by then twenty-four hours had gone by since he had eaten anything, even a serving of vetch.

What to do?

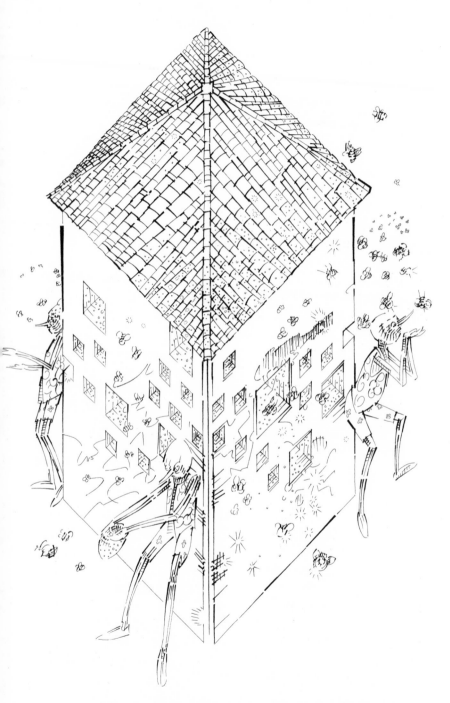

Non gli restavano che due modi per potersi sdigiunare: o chiedere un po' di lavoro, o chiedere in elemosina un soldo o un boccon di pane.

There were only two ways that he could break his fast: either by asking for some work, or begging for a coin or a bite of bread.

He was ashamed to beg, because his father had always taught him that only the elderly and the ill have the right to beg for alms. In this world the truly poor, the ones deserving of aid and compassion, are none other than those who, due to age or sickness, find themselves condemned to no longer be able to earn their bread by the work of their own hands. Everyone else has the duty to work, and if they don't work and they suffer from hunger, all the worse for them.

In the meantime, a man passed by in the street, all sweaty and out of breath. With great difficulty he was pulling two carts full of coal all by himself.

Judging from his appearance that he was a good man, Pinocchio went over to him and, lowering his eyes with shame, whispered:

"Would you be so kind as to give me a coin, since I'm dying of hunger?"

"Not just one coin," answered the coal-seller, "but I'll give you four, provided that you help me pull these two carts of coal home."

"I'm amazed!" answered the puppet, almost offended. "For your information, I've never worked as a donkey; I've never pulled a cart!"

"All the better for you!" answered the coal-seller. Well then, my boy, if you really feel like you're dying of hunger, you can eat two slices of your own arrogance, and take care not to get indigestion."

After a few minutes a mason came along down the road, carrying a bucket of mortar on his shoulders.

"My good man, would you be so kind as to give a coin to a poor boy who is yawning with hunger?"

"With pleasure. Come with me and help carry this mortar," answered the bricklayer, "and instead of one coin, I'll give you five."

"But mortar is heavy," replied Pinocchio, "and I don't want to do hard work."

"Well then, my boy, if you don't want to do hard work, have fun yawning, and much good may it do you."

In less than half an hour twenty more people passed by, and Pinocchio asked all of them for a little offering, but they all answered him:

"Aren't you ashamed of yourself? Instead of loafing around the streets, you'd be better off going to look for some work and learning how to earn your bread!"

Finally a kind little woman carrying two jugs of water passed by.

"Would it be all right with you, kind lady, if I drank a sip of water from your jug?" asked Pinocchio, who was suffering from a burning thirst.

"Of course, my dear boy; drink!" said the little woman, putting the two jugs on the ground.

After Pinocchio had drunk like a sponge, he mumbled under his breath, wiping his mouth:

"I've gotten rid of my thirst! Now if I could only get rid of my hunger!"

Upon hearing these words, the kind little woman quickly added:

"If you help me carry home one of these jugs of water, I'll give you a nice piece of bread."

Pinocchio looked at the jug and answered neither yes nor no.

"And to go with the bread I'll give you a nice dish of cauliflower dressed with oil and vinegar," added the kind woman.

Pinocchio eyed the jug again and answered neither yes nor no.

"And after the cauliflower I'll give you a nice candy filled with *rosolio*."

Seduced by this last delicacy, Pinocchio was no longer able to resist, and, having made up his mind, he said:

"All right, then, I'll bring the jug home for you!"

The jug was quite heavy, and, not having the strength to carry it with his hands, the puppet resigned himself to carrying it on his head.

When they had arrived home, the kind little woman had Pinocchio sit down at a small table that was already set, and she put the bread, the dressed cauliflower, and the candy in front of him.

Pinocchio didn't eat; he gorged himself. His stomach was like an apartment that had been empty and uninhabited for five months.

Once his furious hunger pangs had been, little by little, relieved, he lifted up his head to thank his benefactress; but he hadn't even finished looking at her face when he let out a very long *ooohhhh!* of amazement, and he stood there enchanted, with his eyes wide open, his fork in the air, and his mouth full of bread and cauliflower.

"Whatever is all this amazement about?" asked the kind woman, laughing.

"It's that . . ." answered Pinocchio, stuttering, "it's that . . . it's that . . . you look like . . . you remind me . . . yes, yes, yes, the same voice . . . the same eyes . . . the same hair . . . yes, yes, yes . . . you have blue hair, too . . . like her! . . . Oh my dear little Fairy! . . . Oh my dear little Fairy! . . . Tell me that it's you, really you! . . . Don't make me cry any more! If you only knew! I've cried so much; I've suffered so much! . . ."

And as he said this, Pinocchio wept uncontrollably, and when he had thrown himself to the ground on his knees, he hugged the knees of that mysterious little woman.

CHAPTER TWENTY-FIVE

**Pinocchio promises the Fairy that he will be good
and that he will study, because he's fed up with
being a puppet and he wants to become a good boy.**

*A*T FIRST, THE kind little woman began by saying that she wasn't the little Fairy with the blue hair. But then, seeing that she had already been discovered and not wanting to prolong the comedy, she finally allowed herself to be recognized, and she said to Pinocchio:

"You scamp of a puppet! How did you ever realize it was me?"

"It's the great love that I have for you that told me so."

"Do you remember? You left me when I was a little girl, and now you find me a woman; such a grown woman that I could almost be your mother."

"And that gives me great pleasure, since now instead of calling you my little sister I'll call you my mother. I've yearned for so long to have a mother like all other children! . . . But how did you manage to grow so quickly?"

"It's a secret."

"Teach it to me; I'd like to grow a little, too. Don't you see? I'm still only as tall as a penny's worth of cheese."

"But you can't grow," replied the Fairy.

"Why not?"

"Because puppets never grow. They're born puppets, they live as puppets, and they die as puppets."

"Birba d'un burattino! Come mai ti sei accorto che ero io?"

"Oh! I'm fed up with always being a puppet!" shouted Pinocchio, giving himself a cuff on the head. "It's time that I, too, became a man."

"And you will become one, if you prove that you deserve to . . ."

"Really? And what can I do to deserve to?"

"Something very easy: accustom yourself to being a respectable boy."

"What do you mean — I'm not?"

"Not at all! Respectable boys are obedient, and you, on the other hand . . ."

"And I never obey."

"Respectable boys are fond of studying and working, and you, on the other hand . . ."

"And I, on the other hand, am a loafer and a bum the whole year long."

"Respectable boys always tell the truth . . ."

"And I always tell lies."

"Respectable boys go gladly to school . . ."

"And school gives me a stomachache. But starting today I want to change my life."

"Do you promise me that?"

"I promise. I want to become a respectable little boy, and I want to be a consolation to my father . . . Where can my poor father be now?"

"I don't know."

"Will I ever have the good fortune of being able to see him again and hug him?"

"I believe you will; actually, I'm sure of it."

At this answer Pinocchio's joy was so great and of such magnitude that he took the Fairy's hands and started to kiss them with such fervor that he looked like he was almost out of his mind. Then, lifting his face and looking at her lovingly, he asked:

"Tell me, my little mother: then it's not true that you died?"

"It looks like it's not," answered the Fairy, smiling.

"If you only knew what sorrow I felt, and what a lump I had in my throat, when I read 'here lies' . . ."

"I know; and that's why I've forgiven you. The sincerity of your sorrow made me realize that you have a kind heart, and a boy with a kind heart, even if he's a bit of a rascal and poorly brought up, always leaves some room for hope. I mean, there's always the hope that he'll get back on the right path. And that's the reason why I came looking for you all the way out here. I intend to be your mother . . ."

"Oh! How wonderful!" shouted Pinocchio, jumping with joy.

"You will obey me and you will always do what I tell you to."

"Of course, of course, of course!"

"From tomorrow on," the Fairy continued, "you will start by going to school."

Pinocchio immediately became a little less happy.

"Then you will choose a craft or trade that is to your liking . . ."

Pinocchio became serious.

"What are you grumbling about under your breath?" asked the Fairy with a cross tone.

"I was saying," whined the puppet in a low voice, "that it seems a little late now to be going to school . . ."

"Nossir. Keep in mind that it's never too late to get an education and to learn."

"But I don't want to practice a craft or a trade . . ."

"Why not?"

"Because working seems like a lot of trouble to me."

"My dear boy," said the Fairy, "those who say things like that almost always end up either in jail or in the hospital. For your information, regardless of whether a man is born rich or poor, in this world he's obliged to do something, to have an occupation, to work. Woe to those who fall prey to idleness! Idleness is a terrible illness and needs to be cured immediately, while we're still children, since once we're grown up it can no longer be cured."

These words touched Pinocchio's heart, and, lifting his head brightly, he said to the Fairy:

"I'll study, I'll work, I'll do everything you tell me to, since, when it comes down to it, the puppet's life has begun to bore me, and I want to become a boy at all costs. You promised me that, didn't you?"

"I promised you that, and now it's up to you."

"... e ora dipende da te."

CHAPTER TWENTY-SIX

**Pinocchio goes with his classmates to
the seashore to see the terrible Shark.**

*T*HE NEXT DAY Pinocchio went to the town school.

Imagine those rascally boys when they saw a puppet come into their school! It seemed like the laughter would never end. Everyone played some sort of trick on him: one boy grabbed the cap out of his hand; another pulled his little jacket from behind; one tried to draw a big mustache under his nose with ink; and one even attempted to tie some strings to his feet and hands to make him dance.

For a while Pinocchio kept a nonchalant air and tried to ignore them, but finally, feeling his patience wear thin, he turned to the ones who were pestering him and making the most fun of him and said to them with a dirty look:

"Watch out, boys! I didn't come here to be your buffoon. I respect others and I want to be respected."

"Good for you, booger! You talk like a printed book!" yelled those rascals, doubling over with crazy laughter. And one of them, more impertinent than the others, extended his hand with the intention of grabbing the puppet by the tip of his nose.

But he wasn't quick enough, because Pinocchio stretched his leg out under the table and delivered a kick to the boy's shinbones.

"Bravo berlicche! Hai parlato come un libro stampato!"

"Ouch! What hard feet!" yelled the boy, rubbing the bruise that the puppet had given him.

"And what elbows! . . . Even harder than his feet!" said another one, who had been elbowed in the stomach for his impudent tricks.

The fact of the matter is that after that kick and that elbow jab, Pinocchio immediately won the esteem and favor of all the boys in the school, and they all showered him with a thousand blandishments and loved him with all their hearts.

And even the teacher praised him highly, because he saw that he was attentive, studious, intelligent, always the first to come in to school, always the last to get to his feet at the end of the school day.

The only defect he had was that he hung out with too many of his classmates; and among these there were many rascals who were quite well known for their scarce inclination to study and to distinguish themselves.

The teacher issued him warnings every day, and the good Fairy, too, did not fail to tell him and repeat over and over again:

"Watch out, Pinocchio! Sooner or later those good-for-nothing classmates of yours are going to end up making you lose your love for your studies and maybe even drag you into some big trouble."

"There's no danger of that!" answered the puppet, shrugging his shoulders and tapping the middle of his forehead with his index finger, as if to say: "There's a lot of common sense in here!"

Now it happened that one fine day, as he was walking toward school, he met a pack of those same classmates, who, as they came up to him, said:

"Have you heard the big news?"

"No."

"A Shark as big as a mountain has appeared in the sea near here."

"Really? . . . Could it be that same Shark from when my poor father drowned?"

"We're going to the shore to see him. Do you want to come along with us?"

"Not me. I want to go to school."

"What do you care about school? We'll go to school tomorrow.

"Dunque, via! e chi più corre, è più bravo!"

One class more or one less won't matter; we'll still be the same jackasses as ever."

"And what will the teacher say?"

"Let the teacher say what he wants. He's paid for the express purpose of griping every day."

"And my mother?"

"Mothers never know anything," those devils answered.

"Do you know what I'm going to do?" said Pinocchio. "I want to see the Shark for certain reasons of my own . . . but I'll go see him after school."

"Poor fool!" answered back one of the pack. "You think a fish that big intends to stay there until you're ready for him? As soon as he gets bored, he'll head straight for some other place, and then that'll be the end of that."

"How long does it take to get from here to the beach?" asked the puppet.

"In an hour we'll be there and back."

"Okay, then off we go! And whoever runs the fastest is the best!" shouted Pinocchio.

After the starting signal had thus been given, that pack of rascals, with their books and notebooks under their arms, started to run across the fields, and Pinocchio was always ahead of them all; he seemed to have wings on his feet.

Every now and then he would turn around and poke fun at his classmates, who were at a good distance from him, and when he saw them panting and gasping for breath, covered with dust and with their tongues hanging out, he laughed with all his heart. The unfortunate fellow didn't know at that moment what fearsome and horrible misfortunes were ahead of him!

CHAPTER TWENTY-SEVEN

A great battle between Pinocchio and his
classmates; when one of them gets hurt,
Pinocchio is arrested by the carabinieri.

*W*HEN HE HAD reached the beach, Pinocchio immediately had a long look at the sea, but he didn't see any Shark. The entire sea was as smooth as a huge looking glass.

"So where's the Shark?" he asked, turning to his classmates.

"He must have gone off to have breakfast," answered one of them, laughing.

"Or else he must have jumped into bed for a little nap," added another, laughing harder than ever.

From those senseless answers and that stupid and cruel laughter, Pinocchio understood that his classmates had played a nasty trick on him, since they had given him cause to believe something that wasn't true, and, taking offense, he said to them in an irritated tone:

"And now what? What kind of kick did you get out of making me believe that little story about the Shark?"

"A big kick, you can be sure!" answered those rascals in chorus.

"And what would that be?"

"Making you miss school and come with us. Aren't you ashamed of always appearing so meticulous and diligent in class? Aren't you ashamed of studying as much as you do?"

"And if I study, what does it matter to you?"

"It matters a whole lot to us, because you make us look bad in front of the teacher."

"Why?"

"Because pupils who study always show up the others, like us, who have no desire to study. And we don't want to be shown up! We have our self-esteem, too!"

"And so what do I have to do to satisfy you?"

"You have to get fed up, too, with school, classes, and the teacher, our three great enemies."

"And what if I want to keep studying?"

"We won't look you in the face anymore, and the first chance we get we'll make you pay for it."

"Really, you almost make me laugh," said the puppet with a little shake of his head.

"Hey, Pinocchio!" the biggest of the boys shouted, then, stepping right up to his face. "Don't you come here and swagger; don't you come here and be so cocky! . . . Because you may not be afraid of us, but we're not afraid of you, either! Remember that there's one of you and there are seven of us."

"Seven, like the mortal sins," said Pinocchio with a big laugh.

"Did you hear that? He insulted us all! He called us the seven mortal sins!"

"Pinocchio! Apologize to us for that insult . . . or else you'll be in trouble!"

"Cuckoo!" went the puppet, tapping the tip of his nose with his index finger, in a mocking gesture.

"Pinocchio! This is going to turn out badly for you!"

"Cuckoo!"

"You'll get beaten like a jackass!"

"Cuckoo!"

"You'll go home with a broken nose!"

"Cuckoo!"

"I'll give you a cuckoo now!" shouted the most fearless of those rascals. "Meanwhile, take this down payment, and keep it for tonight's supper."

And saying this, he planted a blow on Pinocchio's head.

But it became, as they say, a sparring match, because the puppet, as was to be expected, immediately responded with another blow. And at that point, from one moment to the next, it became a general and fierce battle.

Although he was alone, Pinocchio defended himself like a hero. With those hard wooden feet of his he managed so well that he was able to keep his enemies at a respectful distance. Wherever his feet could reach and touch, they left the souvenir of a bruise every time.

Then the boys, resentful that they weren't able to compete in hand-to-hand combat with the puppet, decided to lay their hands on their missiles; and once they had undone their bundles of books from school, they started to hurl their spelling primers, grammars, *Giannettinos, Minuzzolos,* Thouar's *Tales,* Baccini's *Little Chick,* and other schoolbooks at him. But the puppet, who had a quick and cunning eye, always ducked his head in time, so that the volumes went right over his head, and all of them ended up falling into the sea.

Imagine the fish! The fish, thinking that those books were something to eat, swarmed quickly to the surface of the water, but after swallowing a few pages or frontispieces, they spat them out again right away, screwing up their mouths in a certain way as if to say: "This is not for us; we're used to being better fed!"

Meanwhile, as the battle grew ever more fierce, a large Crab, who had come out of the water and very slowly crept onto the beach, suddenly shouted in a terrible voice that sounded like a trombone with a cold:

"Cut that out, you little good-for-nothing scamps! These rough wars among boys rarely come to a good end. Something bad always happens!"

Poor Crab! It was as if he had preached to the wind. In fact, that scoundrel Pinocchio, turning around and scowling at him, said rudely:

"Shut up, you tedious Crab! You'd be better off sucking on a couple of lichen drops to cure that sore throat of yours. So go to bed, instead, and try to sweat it off!"

In the meantime the boys, who had by that point finished throwing every last one of their books, caught sight of the puppet's bundle of books lying a short distance away and took possession of them in a flash.

Among these books was a volume bound in thick cardboard, its spine and corners covered in parchment. It was the *Treatise on Arithmetic*. I'll let you imagine how heavy it was!

One of those rascals grabbed the volume, took aim at Pinocchio's head, and slung it with all the strength he had in his arm. But instead of hitting the puppet it hit the head of one of his classmates, who then became as white as a freshly laundered sheet and said nothing more than these words:

"Oh Mother, help me. . . because I'm dying! . . ."

Then he fell flat on the sand.

At the sight of that little dead body, the frightened boys kicked up their heels and raced off, and in a few minutes they were no longer to be seen.

But Pinocchio stayed there; and even if he himself was more dead than alive with grief and fright, he nevertheless ran to soak his handkerchief in seawater and began to bathe his poor classmate's temple. And in the meantime, as he was despairing and weeping uncontrollably, he called his classmate by name and said:

"Eugenio! . . . poor, dear Eugenio! . . . Open your eyes and look at me! . . . Why aren't you answering me? It wasn't me, you know, who hurt you so badly! You've got to believe that it wasn't me! . . . Open your eyes, Eugenio . . . If you keep your eyes closed, you're going to make me die, too . . . Oh my God! How will I be able to go home now? . . . How will I have the courage to present myself to my dear mother? What will become of me? . . . Where will I escape to? . . . Where will I go and hide? . . . Oh! It would have been so much better, a thousand times better, if I had gone to school! . . . Why did I listen to those classmates, who are my damnation? . . . And the teacher had told me so! . . . And my mother had repeated to me: 'Beware of bad company!' But I'm stubborn . . . downright pigheaded . . . I let everyone have their say, but then I always do it my way! And then I'm forced to suffer for it . . . And that's the reason why I haven't had even a quarter hour of peace since I came into the world. My God! What will become of me, what will become of me, what will become of me?"

And Pinocchio kept on crying, bellowing, hitting himself on the head, and calling out poor Eugenio's name, when all of a sudden he heard a muted sound of footsteps drawing near.

He turned around: it was two carabinieri.

"What are you doing lying on the ground there?" they asked Pinocchio.

"I'm assisting this classmate of mine."

"Why? Is he feeling bad?"

"It looks like it!"

"Bad isn't the word for it!" said one of the carabinieri, leaning down and looking at Eugenio closely. "This boy has been wounded in the head; who is it that wounded him?"

"Not me!" stuttered the puppet, who didn't have a breath left in his body.

"If it wasn't you, then who was it that wounded him?"

"Not me!" repeated Pinocchio.

"And what was he wounded with?"

"With this book." And the puppet picked up the *Treatise on Arithmetic*, bound in cardboard and parchment and showed it to the carabiniere.

"And whose book is this?"

"Mine."

"That's enough; we don't need to hear any more. Get up immediately and come with us."

"But I . . ."

"Come with us!"

"But I'm innocent . . ."

"Come with us!"

Before they left, the carabinieri called over some fishermen who at that very moment happened to be going by the beach in their boat and said to them:

"We're going to leave this little boy with a head wound in your custody. Take him home with you and look after him. We'll be back tomorrow to see him."

Then they turned to Pinocchio, and after placing him between them, they ordered in a military tone:

"March! And make it quick or else you'll be in worse trouble!"

Without making them repeat themselves, the puppet began to walk down the path that led to the town. But the poor devil no longer knew what world he was in. He felt like he was dreaming, and what an awful dream! He was beside himself. His eyes saw everything double; his legs trembled; his tongue was stuck to the roof of his mouth and he wasn't able to utter a single word. And yet, in the middle of that dullness and stupor, a terribly sharp worry pierced his heart: the thought, that is, of having to pass by the windows of his good Fairy's house between the carabinieri. He would rather have died.

They had already arrived and were about to enter the town when a violent gust of wind blew off Pinocchio's cap and carried it ten yards or so.

"Would you mind," said the puppet to the carabinieri, "if I went to get my cap?"

"Go ahead, but let's make it quick."

The puppet went off, picked up his cap . . . but instead of putting it on his head, he put it in his mouth, between his teeth, and then started to run at full speed toward the seashore. He shot away like a rifle bullet.

Judging that it would be difficult to catch him, the carabinieri set a large mastiff after him, one that had won first prize in all the dog races. Pinocchio ran, and the dog ran faster; and all the people hung out of their windows and crowded into the street, anxious to see the conclusion to such a ferocious contest.

"Avanti! e cammina spedito! se no, peggio per te!"

But they weren't able to satisfy this desire, because between the mastiff and Pinocchio such a cloud of dust gathered over the street that after a few minutes it was no longer possible to see a thing.

CHAPTER TWENTY-EIGHT

**Pinocchio is in danger of being
fried in a pan like a fish.**

*D*URING THAT desperate race there was one terrible moment, a moment when Pinocchio felt like he was lost. Because you should know that Alidoro (that was the mastiff's name),
after running and running, had almost caught up with him.

Suffice it to say that the puppet could hear that dreadful beast's
labored panting at a palm's length behind him, and he could
even feel the rush of his hot breath.

It was his good luck that the beach was at this point close by
and the sea visible a few paces away.

As soon as he got to the beach, the puppet took a wonderful
leap, like a frog might have done, and ended up falling right into
the water. Alidoro, on the other hand, wanted to stop, but trans-
ported by the heat of the race, he, too, went into the water. And
since that poor wretch didn't know how to swim, he immediately
started to flounder about with his paws in an attempt to stay afloat.
But the more he floundered the more his head went underwater.

When he managed to get his head above water again, the poor
dog's eyes were rolling with fright. Barking, he shouted:

"I'm drowning! I'm drowning!"

"Drop dead!" Pinocchio answered from afar, since by that
point he saw that he was safe from any danger.

"Help me, my dear Pinocchio! . . . save me from death!"

At those excruciating shrieks, the puppet, who, when it came down to it, had an excellent heart, was moved to compassion, and turning to the dog said:

"But if I help save you, will you promise not to bother me anymore and to stop running after me?"

"I promise! I promise! Hurry up, for goodness' sake! If you take another half minute, I'll already be dead."

Pinocchio hesitated for a moment, but then, remembering how many times his father had told him that a good deed is never regretted, swam over to Alidoro and taking him by the tail with both hands pulled him, safe and sound, onto the dry sand of the beach.

The poor dog could no longer stand on his legs. Without meaning to, he had drunk so much salt water that he was as swollen as a balloon. For his part, the puppet, who didn't feel like trusting the dog too much, decided that it would be prudent to throw himself back into the sea, and as he got farther and farther from the shore, he shouted to the friend that he had saved:

"Good-bye, Alidoro; have a good trip and give my best to everyone at home."

"Good-bye, Pinocchio," answered the dog; "a thousand thanks for having freed me from death. You did me a great favor, and in this world you give as good as you get. If the opportunity presents itself, we'll take this up again . . ."

Pinocchio continued to swim, always keeping close to land. Finally he seemed to have reached a safe place, and when he glanced toward the shore, up on the cliffs he saw a sort of grotto, from which a very long plume of smoke was issuing.

"There must be a fire in that grotto," he said to himself. "So much the better! I'll go get dry and warm up, and then what? . . . and then whatever will be will be."

When he had made this resolution, he drew up closer to the rocks. But just as he was about to start climbing up, he felt something under the water that was pulling him up, up, until he was in the air. He immediately tried to escape, but at that point it was too late, because to his great surprise he found himself enclosed in a large net, in the company of a mass of fish of every size and shape that squirmed and thrashed about like desperate souls.

And at the same time he saw a fisherman come out of the grotto, a fisherman who was so ugly, so terribly ugly, that he looked like a sea monster. On his head he had a dense thicket of green grasses in the place of hair; the skin on his body was green; his eyes were green; his long beard, which went all the way down to here, was green. He looked like a huge lizard sitting up on its hind feet.

When the fisherman had pulled his net from the sea, he shouted, quite happy:

"Bless the heavens! I'll be able to have a fine feast of fish again today!"

"Good that I'm not a fish," said Pinocchio to himself, getting back a little of his courage.

The net full of fish was taken into the grotto, a dark and smoky grotto in the middle of which was sizzling a large frying pan of oil that gave off a little snufflike odor that was enough to take away your breath.

"Now let's take a look and see what kind of fish we've got!" said the green fisherman. And into the net he thrust a hand so enormous that it looked like a baker's peel, and pulled out a handful of red mullet.

"Good, these red mullet!" he said, looking at them and sniffing them with satisfaction. And after he had sniffed them, he flung them into a large basin without any water in it.

Then he repeated the same operation over and over again, and as he extracted the other fish he could feel his mouth watering, and, beside himself with delight, he said:

"Good, these hake!

"Exquisite, these mullet!

"Delicious, these sole!

"Choice, these sting-bull!

"Adorable, these anchovies with their heads still on!"

As you can imagine, the hake, mullet, sole, sting-bull, and anchovies all went haphazardly into the basin to keep the red mullet company.

The last one to remain in the net was Pinocchio.

As soon as the fisherman had pulled him out, he opened his big green eyes wide with wonder and yelled out, nearly in a fright:

"What kind of fish is this? I don't remember ever having eaten a fish that looked like this!"

And he looked carefully at Pinocchio again, and, after having looked at him from every angle, he concluded:

"I see: it must be a sea crab."

Then Pinocchio, who was mortified to hear himself mistaken for a crab, said in a resentful tone:

"What do you mean, a crab? You be careful how you treat me! For your information, I'm a puppet."

"A puppet?" replied the fisherman. "To tell you the truth, the puppet fish is a new fish for me! Even better! I'll eat you with more gusto."

"Eat me? Don't you understand that I'm not a fish? Or can't you hear that I'm talking and reasoning, just like you?"

"That's quite true," the fisherman went on, "and since I can see that you're a fish that has the good fortune to talk and reason just like me, I want to show you the regard that is due you."

"And what would this regard be?"

"As a sign of my friendship and particular esteem for you, I'll leave the choice of how you want to be cooked up to you. Would you like to be fried in a pan, or would you prefer to be cooked in a skillet with some tomato sauce?"

"To tell you the truth," answered Pinocchio, "if I have to choose, I would prefer to be left free, so that I can go back home."

"You're joking! Does it look to you like I want to lose the opportunity to taste such a rare fish? A puppet fish certainly doesn't turn up every day in these seas. Leave it to me: I'll fry you in the pan together with all the other fish, and you'll see that you'll like it. It's always a comfort to be fried in good company."

When he heard this sad tune, the unhappy Pinocchio began to cry, scream, and beg for mercy, and as he was crying he said: "It would have been so much better if I had gone to school! . . . I wanted to listen to my classmates, and now I'm paying for it! Boo hoo hoo!"

And since he was wriggling like an eel and making incredible efforts to slip out of the green fisherman's clutches, the latter took some nice rushes and, after he had tied the puppet's hands and feet together like a salami, threw him to the bottom of the basin with the others.

Then he pulled out a beat-up wooden tray that was full of flour and set about dredging all those fish; and once he had dredged them, he threw them into the pan to fry.

The first ones to start dancing in the boiling oil were the poor hake; the sting-bull were next, then the mullet, then the sole and the anchovies. And then it was Pinocchio's turn. When he saw himself so close to death (and what an awful death!) he was overcome by such trembling and such fright that he no longer had either the voice or the breath to beg for mercy.

The poor child begged for mercy with his eyes! But the green fisherman, without paying him the least attention, rolled him five or six times in the flour until he was dredged so thoroughly from head to toe that it looked like he had become a plaster puppet.

Then he took Pinocchio by the head, and . . .

. . . infarinandolo così bene . . . che pareva diventato
un burattino di gesso. Poi lo prese per il capo, e . . .

CHAPTER TWENTY-NINE

**He returns to the house of the Fairy,
who promises him that the next day he
will no longer be a puppet but will
become a boy. Grand breakfast of coffee-
and-milk to celebrate this great event.**

*J*UST AS THE FISHERMAN was about to throw Pinocchio
into the frying pan, into the cave entered a large dog that had
been led there by the strong, mouthwatering smell of the fish fry.

"Get out of here!" yelled the fisherman, threatening the dog
while still holding the dredged puppet in his hand.

But the poor dog had enough appetite for four, and, whim-
pering and wagging his tail, he seemed to be saying:

"Give me a bite of the fry and I'll leave you in peace."

"Get out of here, I said!" the fisherman repeated, and extended his leg to give him a kick.

Then the dog, who when he was truly hungry wasn't accus-
tomed to letting even so much as a fly land on his nose, turned to
the fisherman and snarled, showing him his terrible fangs.

At that same moment a weak, faint little voice was heard in the
cave, and it said:

"Save me, Alidoro! If you don't save me, I'm fried!"

The dog immediately recognized Pinocchio's voice and realized to his great amazement that the little voice had come out of
that dredged bundle that the fisherman had in his hand.

So what does he do? With a great leap he bounds up from the ground, grabs the floured bundle in his mouth, and, holding it gently between his teeth, runs out of the grotto and is off in a flash!

The fisherman, quite angry to see snatched from his hands a fish that he would so gladly have eaten, tried to run after the dog. But after taking a few steps, he had a coughing fit and had to go back.

In the meantime Alidoro, who had found the path that led back to town, stopped and delicately placed his friend Pinocchio on the ground.

"I owe you a lot of thanks!" said the puppet.

"No need for that," replied the dog, "you saved me, and you give as good as you get. Everyone knows that: in this world we've all got to help each other."

"But how did you end up in that grotto?"

"I was still lying here on the beach, more dead than alive, when the wind brought me an enticing little smell of fish fry from far away. That little smell whet my appetite, and I followed it. If I had arrived a minute later! . . ."

"Don't say that!" howled Pinocchio, who was still shaking from fear. "Don't say that! If you had arrived a minute later, right now I'd already be fried, eaten, and digested! Brrr! Just thinking about it gives me the shivers!"

Alidoro, laughing, extended his right paw to the puppet, who squeezed it tightly in token of their great friendship, and then they parted ways.

The dog set off on his way home, and Pinocchio, once he was alone, went to a hut not far from there and asked a little old man who was sitting at the door warming himself in the sun:

"Tell me, my good man, do you know anything about a poor boy named Eugenio who was wounded in the head?"

"The boy was brought to this hut by some fishermen, and now . . ."

"Now he must be dead!" interrupted Pinocchio, with great sorrow.

"No; now he's alive, and he has already gone back home."

"Really? Really?" shouted the puppet, jumping for joy, "so it wasn't a serious wound?"

"But it could have been very serious, even fatal," answered the little old man, "because they hit him in the head with a big cardboard-bound book."

"And who hit him with it?"

"A schoolmate of his: a certain Pinocchio . . ."

"And who is this Pinocchio?" asked the puppet, playing dumb.

"They say he's a bad boy, a bum, a real madcap . . ."

"Lies! They're all lies!"

"Do you know him, this Pinocchio?"

"By sight!" answered the puppet.

"And what's your opinion of him?" the little old man asked.

"He seems to me to be a very good child, full of desire to study, obedient, fond of his father and his family . . ."

While the puppet was cheekily churning out all of these lies, he touched his nose and realized that it had grown more than a palm's length longer. Then, quite frightened, he started to shout:

"Don't listen, my fine man, to any of the good things I told you about him, because I know Pinocchio very well and I, too, can assure you that he is truly a bad boy, disobedient and lazy, who instead of going to school goes and plays mischief with his schoolmates!"

As soon as he had uttered these words, his nose grew shorter and returned to its natural size, as it had been before.

"And why are you all white like that?" the little old man asked him all of a sudden.

"I'll tell you . . . without realizing what I was doing, I rubbed against a wall that had just been painted," answered the puppet, since he was ashamed to tell of how he had been dredged in flour like a fish so that he could be fried in a pan.

"And what did you do with your jacket, your trousers, and your cap?"

"I met up with some thieves and they stripped me. Tell me, my good old man, would you by chance have some scraps of clothing to give me, just so that I can get back home?"

"My dear boy, as far as clothes go, all I have is a little sack where I keep beans. If you want it, you can take it: there it is, over there."

Pinocchio didn't need to be told twice: he went right over and took the bean sack, which was empty, made a little hole at the bottom and two holes on the sides with some scissors, and slipped it over his head like a shirt. And lightly dressed like that, he set off for town.

But along the way he was not feeling at all calm; in fact, he took one step forward and then one backward, and discussing with himself, he said:

"How am I going to present myself to my dear little Fairy? What will she say when she sees me? . . . Will she be willing to forgive this second escapade of mine? . . . I bet she won't forgive me! . . . Oh! Of course she won't forgive me . . . And that serves me right, because I'm a rascal and I always promise to reform my ways, and I never keep those promises!"

When he got to town it was already the middle of the night, and since the weather was awful and the rain was coming down in buckets, he went straight to the Fairy's house, with his mind set on knocking at the door until it was opened.

But when he got there he felt his courage waning, and, instead of knocking, he ran off until he was about twenty paces away. Then he went back to the door a second time, but nothing came of it; then he went up a third time, and nothing. The fourth time he took hold of the iron knocker and, trembling, gave a tiny little knock.

He waited and waited, and finally after half an hour a window on the top floor opened (the house had four floors) and Pinocchio saw that a large snail with a small lamp burning on her head was looking out. She asked:

"Who is it, at this hour?"

"Is the Fairy home?" asked the puppet.

"The Fairy is asleep and doesn't want to be awakened; who are you, anyway?"

"It's me!"

"Who's me?"

"Pinocchio."

"Pinocchio who?"

"The puppet, the one who lives with the Fairy."

"Oh! I see," said the Snail, "wait for me where you are; I'll come down right now to open up for you."

"For goodness' sake, be quick about it, because I'm freezing to death."

"My dear boy, I'm a snail, and snails are never in a hurry."

Meanwhile, an hour went by, two hours went by, and the door wasn't opening. And so Pinocchio, who was shivering from cold, fear, and the water that was covering him, gathered up his courage and knocked a second time, and this time he knocked harder.

At that second knock a window on the floor below opened and the same snail looked out.

"Pretty little Snail," shouted Pinocchio from the street, "I've been waiting for two hours! And two hours, on a miserable evening like this, become longer than two years. Make it quick, for goodness' sake."

"My dear boy," answered that little creature from the window, all calm and composed, "my dear boy, I'm a snail, and snails are never in a hurry."

And the window closed again.

A short time later the bells rang midnight; then one, then two in the morning, and the door was still closed.

At that point Pinocchio, having lost his patience, angrily grabbed the knocker with the intention of giving it a blow that would make the whole building shake. But the knocker, which was made of iron, suddenly became a live eel, which wriggled out of his hands and disappeared into a trickle of water that was running down the middle of the street.

"Spicciatevi, per carità."

"Alright then!" shouted Pinocchio, ever more blinded by his rage. "If the knocker has disappeared, then I'll keep on knocking with my feet."

And he moved back a little and then gave the front door an almighty kick. The blow was so strong that half of his foot went through the wood, and when the puppet tried to pull it back out, it was an utterly wasted effort, for his foot had remained stuck in the door, like a riveted nail.

Imagine poor Pinocchio! He had to spend the whole rest of the night with one foot on the ground and that other one in the air.

In the morning, as it was getting light, the door finally opened. It had taken the Snail, that fine little animal, only nine hours to descend from the fourth floor to the front door. You could say that she had worked up a good sweat!

"What are you doing with that foot of yours stuck in the door?" she asked the puppet, laughing.

"I've had an accident. Pretty little Snail, see if you can manage to free me from this agony."

"My dear boy, you need a carpenter to do that, and I've never practiced the carpenter's trade."

"Beg the Fairy for me!"

"The Fairy is asleep and doesn't want to be awakened."

"But what do you expect me to do, nailed all day to this door?"

"Amuse yourself by counting the ants that go by on the street."

"At least bring me something to eat, since I'm feeling worn out."

"Right away!" said the Snail.

In fact, after three and a half hours Pinocchio saw her coming back with a silver tray on her head. On the tray there was bread, a roast chicken, and four ripe apricots.

"Here's the lunch the Fairy sends you," said the Snail.

At the sight of all those good things, the puppet cheered right up. But what a great disappointment when, as he started to eat, he realized that the bread was made of plaster, the chicken of cardboard, and the four apricots, colored as if they were real, of alabaster.

He wanted to cry, he wanted to give in to despair, he wanted to throw away the tray and what was on it. But instead, either because of his great pain or his great weakness of stomach, the fact of the matter is that he fainted.

When he came to, he found himself stretched out on a sofa, and the Fairy was next to him.

"I'll forgive you this time, too," the Fairy said to him, "but you'll be in trouble if you try to play another one of your tricks on me!"

Pinocchio promised and swore that he would study and that he would always behave well. And he kept his word for the whole rest of the year. In fact, at the exams before vacation, he had the honor of being the best in the school, and his conduct was, in general, judged to be so praiseworthy and satisfactory that the Fairy, quite happy, said to him:

"Tomorrow your wish will finally be granted!"

"What do you mean?"

"Tomorrow you'll stop being a wooden puppet, and you'll become a respectable boy."

Those who didn't see Pinocchio's joy upon hearing this much-longed-for news will never be able to imagine it. All his friends and schoolmates were to be invited to a grand breakfast the next day at the Fairy's house to celebrate the great event all together, and the Fairy had ordered two hundred cups of coffee-and-milk and four hundred rolls, buttered on both sides, to be made. That day promised to be quite lovely and quite happy, but . . .

Unfortunately, in the life of puppets there's always a "but" that ruins everything.

CHAPTER THIRTY

**Instead of becoming a boy, Pinocchio secretly
leaves for Playland with his friend Lampwick.**

*A*s IS ONLY natural, Pinocchio immediately asked the
Fairy for permission to go around town and invite everyone,
and the Fairy said to him:

"By all means, go and invite your schoolmates for tomorrow's
breakfast. But remember to come back home before night falls.
Do you understand?"

"I promise that I'll be back in just an hour," replied the puppet.

"Be careful, Pinocchio! Children are quick to make promises,
but most of the time they're slow to keep them."

"But I'm not like others. When I say something, I keep my word."

"We'll see. If by chance you disobey me, all the worse for you."

"Why?"

"Because children who don't listen to the advice of those who
know more than they do always meet up with some misfortune."

"And I've had that very experience!" said Pinocchio. "But now
I'm not going to make the same mistake again!"

"We'll see if you're telling the truth."

Without adding another word, the puppet said good-bye to his
good Fairy, who was like a mother to him, and he went out the
front door singing and dancing.

In just over an hour, all of his friends were invited. Some accepted right away and wholeheartedly; others needed to be begged

a bit, at first. But when they found out that the rolls to be dipped in the coffee-and-milk would also be buttered on the outside, they all ended up saying: "We'll come, too, to make you happy."

Now you should know that among Pinocchio's friends and schoolmates, there was one who was his favorite and very dear to him. This boy's name was Romeo, but everyone called him by his nickname, Lampwick, on account of his lean, spare, and lanky little body, which looked exactly like a new wick on an oil lamp.

Lampwick was the laziest and most mischievous boy in the whole school, but Pinocchio adored him. And in fact, he immediately went to look for him at his house, so that he could invite him to the breakfast, but he didn't find him. He went back a second time, and Lampwick wasn't there. He went back a third time, and his trip was in vain.

Where could he track him down? He looked here and he looked there until he finally found him hiding under the portico of a farmer's house.

"What are you doing under there?" Pinocchio asked, going up to him.

"I'm waiting to leave . . ."

"Where are you going?"

"Far, far, far away!"

"You know, I came looking for you at your house three times!"

"What did you want with me?"

"Don't you know about the great event? Don't you know about the good luck I've had?"

"What good luck?"

"Tomorrow I stop being a puppet and I become a boy like you and all the other boys."

"Much good may it do you."

"So, then, tomorrow I'll expect you for breakfast at my house."

"But I'm telling you that I'm leaving tonight."

"At what time?"

"In a little while."

"And where are you going?"

"I'm going to live in a town . . . that is the most wonderful town in this world: a real land of plenty."

"And what's it called?"

"It's called Playland. Why don't you come, too?"

"Me? No, I couldn't!"

"You're doing the wrong thing, Pinocchio! Believe me, if you don't come, you'll be sorry. Where do you think you can find a healthier town for us kids? There are no schools there; there are no teachers; there are no books. In that blessed town no one ever studies. Thursdays there's no school, and every week is made up of six Thursdays and a Sunday. Just imagine, winter vacation starts on the first of January and ends the last day of December. That's the kind of town I really like! That's how all civilized towns should be!"

"But how do they spend their days in Playland?"

"They spend them playing and having fun from morning till night. Then at night they go to bed, and in the morning they start all over again. What do you think?"

"Hmmm . . ." went Pinocchio, and he shook his head a little, as if to say: "That's a life I'd gladly live, too!"

"So, do you want to leave with me? Yes or no? Make up your mind."

"No, no, no, and no again. I've already promised my good Fairy that I'll become a respectable boy, and I want to keep the promise. In fact, since I see the sun is going down, I'm going to leave you right away and be off. So good-bye, and have a good trip."

"Where are you running off to in such a hurry?"

"Home. My good Fairy wants me to come back before night."

"Wait two more minutes."

"I'll be too late."

"Just two minutes."

"And then what if the Fairy yells at me ?"

"Let her yell. When she's yelled nice and long, she'll quiet down," said that scamp Lampwick.

"And how are you going to do this? Are you going by yourself or with others?"

"By myself? There'll be more than a hundred boys."

"And are you traveling on foot?"

"In a little while a carriage will be passing by here to pick me up and take me all the way to the border of that delightful town."

"I'd sure pay a lot to have the carriage pass by right now!"

"Why?"

"So that I could see you all leave together."

"Stay a little longer and you'll see us."

"No, no. I want to go back home."

"Wait two more minutes."

"I've taken too long as it is. The Fairy will be worrying about me."

"Poor Fairy! Maybe she's afraid that the bats are going to eat you?"

"So, then," resumed Pinocchio, "are you really sure there are no schools in that town?"

"Not even the shadow of one."

"And no teachers, either?"

"Not a one."

"And you never have to study?"

"Never, never, never!"

"What a lovely town!" said Pinocchio, feeling his mouth start to water. "What a lovely town! I've never been there, but I can imagine it!"

"Why don't you come, too?"

"There's no point in you trying to tempt me! I've already promised my good Fairy that I'll become a sensible boy, and I don't want to go back on my word."

"Well, then, good-bye, and give my very best to the grammar schools and to the high schools, too, if you meet up with them on the road."

"Good-bye, Lampwick; have a good trip, have fun and remember your friends now and then."

When he had said this, the puppet took two steps, as if to leave. But then he stopped, turned to his friend, and asked him:

"But are you really sure that in that town the weeks are all made up of six Thursdays and a Sunday?"

"Quite sure."

"But are you certain that vacation starts on the first of January and ends the last day of December?"

"Quite certain."

"What a lovely town!" repeated Pinocchio, spitting with uncontainable joy. Then, having made up his mind, he added, in a great hurry:

"So good-bye then, for real, and have a good trip."

"Good-bye."

"In how long will you be leaving?"

"In a little while!"

"Too bad! I just might be able to wait."

"And what about the Fairy?"

"I'm already late! And it'll be all the same if I go home an hour earlier or later."

"Poor Pinocchio! And what if the Fairy yells at you?"

"Never mind! I'll let her yell. When she's yelled nice and long, she'll quiet down."

Meanwhile night had already fallen, and a dark night it was. Then all of a sudden they saw a little light moving in the distance . . . and they heard the sound of harness bells and the blare of a trumpet, so faint and stifled that it sounded like the buzzing of a mosquito!

"Here it is," yelled Lampwick, getting to his feet.

"Who is it?" asked Pinocchio under his breath.

"It's the carriage that's come to get me. So do you want to come, yes or no?"

"But is it really true," asked the puppet, "that in that town kids never have to study?"

"Never, never, never!"

"What a lovely town! . . . What a lovely town! . . . What a lovely town!"

"Che bel paese! . . . che bel paese! . . . che bel paese!. . ."

CHAPTER THIRTY-ONE

**After five months of fun and games Pinocchio,
to his great surprise, finds himself sprouting
a lovely pair of asinine ears, and he becomes
a little donkey, tail and all.**

FINALLY THE CARRIAGE arrived, and it arrived without making the slightest sound, because its wheels were wrapped in tow and rags.

It was pulled by twelve pairs of little donkeys, all the same size, but with different colored coats.

Some were gray, others white, others salt-and-pepper, and others had big yellow and blue stripes.

But the most unusual thing was this: that those twelve pairs, or, as it were, twenty-four little donkeys, instead of being shod like all other beasts of burden or labor, wore men's little white leather boots on their feet.

And the driver of the carriage?

Imagine a little man, wider than he is tall, as soft and greasy as a pat of butter, with a little face like a rose-apple, a little mouth that was always laughing, and a delicate and caressing voice, like that of a cat trying to appeal to the good heart of its mistress.

As soon as they saw him, all the boys fell in love with him and raced each other to hop up onto his carriage, so that he could take them off to that authentic land of plenty known on maps by the seductive name of Playland.

In fact, the carriage was already completely full of little boys between eight and twelve years old, piled up on top of each other like so many salted anchovies. They were uncomfortable, they were crushed, they could barely breathe, but no one said *ouch!* and no one complained. The consolation of knowing that in a few hours they would arrive in a town where there were neither books nor schools nor teachers made them so happy and accepting that they felt neither discomfort nor exhaustion nor hunger nor thirst nor sleepiness.

As soon as the carriage stopped, the Little Man turned to Lampwick and, with a thousand blandishments and a thousand little affectations, asked him, smiling:

"Tell me, my lovely boy, do you want to come to that fair town, too?"

"Sure I want to come."

"But I need to let you know, my little dear, that there's no room left in the carriage. As you can see, it's completely full!"

"Oh well!" replied Lampwick, "If there's no room left in the carriage, I'll make do with sitting on the wheel shafts."

And with a leap, he landed on the wheel shaft and straddled it.

"And you, my love?" said the Little Man, turning to Pinocchio, all full of polite attention, "what do you intend to do? Are you coming with us, or are you staying?"

"I'm staying," answered Pinocchio. "I want to go back home; I want to study and I want to distinguish myself at school, like all respectable children do."

"Much good may it do you!"

"Pinocchio!" Lampwick said, then. "Listen to me: come with us, and we'll have a merry time."

"No, no, no!"

"Come with us and we'll be merry!" a hundred voices shouted all together from inside the carriage.

"And if I come with you, what will my good Fairy say?" said the puppet, who was beginning to soften up and vacillate.

"Don't trouble yourself with such gloomy thoughts. Just think, we're going to a town where we'll be free to make a racket from morning till night!"

Pinocchio didn't answer, but he sighed, and then he sighed again, and then he sighed a third time. Finally he said:

"Make a little room for me: I want to come, too!"

"The seats are all taken," replied the Little Man, "but just to show you how welcome you are, I can let you have my seat, up here in the box . . ."

"And what about you?"

"I'll come along on foot."

"No, I really can't allow you to do that. I'd rather jump on the back of one of these little donkeys!" yelled Pinocchio.

No sooner said than done. He went over to the right-hand donkey of the first pair and made as if to get on it. But the little animal turned around suddenly and butted him hard in the stomach, which left him on the ground with his feet in the air.

Imagine the impertinent and raucous howls of laughter of all those boys who witnessed the scene.

But the Little Man didn't laugh. Full of lovingness, he drew close to the little rebel donkey and, pretending to give him a kiss, bit off half of his right ear.

Meanwhile Pinocchio, getting up from the ground in a rage, sprung back onto the back of that poor animal with a leap. And it was such a fine leap that the other boys, once they had stopped laughing, began to yell "Long live Pinocchio!" and to clap their hands so long and loud that it seemed they would never stop.

When all of a sudden the little donkey lifted both of his hind legs and, bucking as hard as he could, hurled the poor puppet onto a pile of gravel in the middle of the road.

Wild laughter, then, all over again; but the Little Man, instead of laughing, felt himself overwhelmed by so much love for that restless little ass that, with a kiss, he did cleanly away with half of the other ear. Then he said to the puppet:

"You can get back on now, and don't be afraid. That little donkey had a bee in his bonnet, but I whispered two little words

. . . ma la bestiòla, voltandosi a secco, gli dètte una
gran musata nello stomaco e lo gettò a gambe all'aria.

in his ear and I hope that I've tamed him down and made him more reasonable."

Pinocchio got on, and the carriage began to move. But while the little donkeys were galloping and the carriage was traveling along the cobblestones of the main road, the puppet seemed to hear a soft, barely audible voice that said to him:

"Poor ninny! You wanted to do things your way, but you'll be sorry!"

Pinocchio, a bit frightened, looked this way and that, trying to figure out where those words were coming from. But he didn't see anyone: the little donkeys were galloping, the carriage was traveling along, the boys inside the carriage were sleeping, Lampwick was snoring as if he were sawing logs, and the Little Man, sitting in his box, was singing softly through his teeth:

> Everyone sleeps at night
> But I, I never sleep . . .

After they had gone a quarter of a mile, Pinocchio heard the same little faint voice that said:

"Keep this in mind, you little fool! Children who quit studying and turn their backs on books, schools, and teachers so that they can devote themselves entirely to fun and games can only come to a bad end! . . . I know it from experience! . . . And I can tell you about it! A day will come when you'll be crying, too, just like I'm crying today . . . but then it will be too late!"

At these words, which were whispered softly, the puppet, more and more frightened, jumped down from his mount and went to take his little donkey by the muzzle.

And imagine how surprised he was when he realized that his little donkey was crying . . . and he was crying just like a child!

"Hey, Mister Little Man," shouted Pinocchio, then, to the owner of the carriage. "You know what's new? This little donkey is crying."

"Let him cry; he'll laugh when he gets married."

"But maybe you've also taught him to speak?"

"No; he learned to mumble a few words by himself, since he spent three years in a company of trained dogs."

"Poor animal!"

"Come on, come on, now," said the Little Man, "let's not waste our time watching a donkey cry. Get back on, and let's go; the night is cool and the road is long."

Pinocchio obeyed without saying another word. The carriage continued its journey and the next morning, at the break of dawn, they happily arrived in Playland.

This town resembled no other town in the world. Its population was composed entirely of boys: the oldest were fourteen, the youngest barely eight. In the streets there was enough merrymaking, enough racket, enough shrieking to drive you crazy! Packs of rascals everywhere: some were playing the walnut game and some were playing jacks; some were playing ball; some were riding velocipedes and some were on wooden horses; some were playing blindman's bluff and others tag; yet others, dressed as clowns, were swallowing burning tow; some were reciting lines and some were singing; some were doing flips; some were amusing themselves by walking on their hands with their feet in the air; some were rolling hoops and some were walking around dressed as generals, with leaf helmets and papier-mâché sabers; some were laughing and some shouting, some calling others, some clapping their hands, some whistling and some making the sound of a chicken when it lays an egg. In short, there was such pandemonium, such squawking, such an infernal noise that you had to put cotton in your ears if you didn't want to go deaf. In all of the squares you could see canvas puppet theaters, crowded with boys from morning till night, and on the sides of all the houses you could read lovely things written in charcoal, such as: "Long live toies!" (instead of "toys"); "No more skules!" (instead of "no more schools"); "Down with A Rith Mitik" (instead of "arithmetic"), and other similar gems.

As soon as they had set foot in the town, Pinocchio, Lampwick,

In mezzo ai continui spassi . . . le ore, i giorni,
le settimane passavano come tanti baleni.

and all the other boys that had taken the trip with the Little Man threw themselves right into the great bustle, and in a few minutes, as can easily be imagined, they had become everyone's friends. Who could have been happier or more content than they were?

In the midst of the nonstop fun and the diverse amusements, the hours, the days, and the weeks passed by in a flash.

"Oh, what a lovely life!" Pinocchio would say every time he happened to run into Lampwick.

"You see, then; wasn't I right?" the latter chided him. "And to think that you didn't want to come along! And to think that you had gotten it into your head to go back home to your Fairy, so that you could waste your time studying! . . . If you're free of the bother of books and schools today, you owe it to me, to my advice, to my attention; won't you admit that? True friends are the only ones that know how to do such great favors."

"It's true, Lampwick! If I'm a truly happy boy today it's all thanks to you. But you know what the teacher used to tell me when he was talking about you? He always used to tell me: 'Don't associate with that scoundrel Lampwick, because Lampwick is a bad influence, and the only advice you'll ever get from him is to be bad!'"

"Poor teacher!" replied the other boy, shaking his head. "I know, unfortunately, that I irritated him and that he used to amuse himself by slandering me, but I'm generous and I forgive him!"

"What a great soul!" said Pinocchio, hugging his friend affectionately and giving him a kiss between his eyes.

In the meantime, five months had already gone by since they had begun this lovely pastime of playing and having fun all day, without ever laying eyes on either a book or a school. Then one morning, upon awakening, Pinocchio had, as they say, one heck of an awful surprise, which put him into quite a bad mood.

CHAPTER THIRTY-TWO

Pinocchio gets donkey ears, and then he becomes a real donkey and starts to bray.

*A*ND WHAT WAS this surprise?

I'll tell you, my dear little readers: the surprise was that Pinocchio, upon awakening, felt the natural urge to scratch his head, and while scratching his head he realized . . .

Go ahead and guess what he realized!

He realized, to his enormous astonishment, that his ears had grown more than a palm's length.

You know that the puppet had had tiny little ears ever since birth: so tiny that they weren't even visible to the naked eye! So imagine how surprised he was when he was forced to feel with his own hands that during the night his ears had grown so long that they looked like two rush dusters.

He went right off in search of a mirror so that he could look at himself, but since he couldn't find a mirror, he filled the hand basin with water and, looking at his reflection in it, saw what he never would have wished to see: he saw, that is, his own image embellished by a magnificent pair of asinine ears.

I'll let you imagine the pain, the shame, and the desperation of poor Pinocchio!

He began to cry, to shriek, to bang his head on the wall, but the more he despaired, the more his ears grew, and grew, and grew, and became hairy toward the tips.

At the sound of those piercing cries, a lovely Little Groundhog that lived on the floor above came into the room. When she saw the puppet in such a frenzy, she asked him kindly:

"What's the matter, my dear neighbor?"

"I'm ill, my Little Groundhog, very ill . . . and ill with an illness that frightens me! Do you know how to take a pulse?"

"Just a little."

"Then check if by chance I've got a fever."

The Little Groundhog lifted up her front paw, and after having felt Pinocchio's pulse, she said to him, sighing:

"My friend, I'm sorry to have to give you some bad news!"

"What is it?"

"You have one nasty fever!"

"And what type of fever would that be?"

"Donkey fever."

"I don't understand this fever!" answered the puppet, who had, unfortunately, understood.

"Then I'll explain it to you," continued the Little Groundhog. "You should know, then, that in two or three hours you will be neither a puppet nor a boy . . ."

"And what will I be?"

"In two or three hours, you will become a real live little donkey, like the ones that pull carts and bring cabbage and lettuce to the market."

"Oh! Poor me! Poor me!" shouted Pinocchio, grabbing his ears with both hands and pulling and tearing at them in a rage, as if they were someone else's ears.

"My dear," replied the Little Groundhog, trying to console him, "what can you do about it? At this point it's destiny. At this point it's written in the decrees of wisdom that all lazy boys who get fed up with books, schools, and teachers and spend their days in fun and games and other amusements sooner or later must end up being transformed into so many little jackasses."

"But is it really just like that?" asked the puppet, sobbing.

"Unfortunately, it is! And crying serves no purpose now. You should have thought of it before!"

"But it's not my fault. Believe me, Little Groundhog, it's all Lampwick's fault!"

"And who is this Lampwick?"

"A schoolmate of mine. I wanted to go home; I wanted to be obedient; I wanted to keep on studying and distinguish myself . . . but Lampwick said to me: 'Why do you want to bother yourself with study? Why do you want to go to school? . . . Come with me to Playland instead; we won't have to study anymore, we'll have a great time from morning till night, and we'll always be happy.'"

"And why did you follow the advice of that false friend? Of that bad companion?"

"Why? . . . Because, my Little Groundhog, I'm a puppet without common sense . . . and without a heart. Oh! If I had had just a tiny bit of a heart, I would never have abandoned that good Fairy, who loved me like a mother and did so much for me! . . . And right now I wouldn't be a puppet anymore . . . but instead I'd be a respectable little boy, like so many others! Oh! But if I meet up with Lampwick, he'll be in trouble! I'm going to beat the tar out of him!"

And he made as if to go out. But when he was at the door, he remembered that he had ass's ears, and since he was ashamed of showing them in public, what did he invent? He took a big cotton cap and, after sticking it on his head, he pulled it all the way down to the tip of his nose.

Then he went out and set about looking all over for Lampwick. He looked for him in the streets, in the squares, in the puppet theaters, every place, but he didn't find him. He asked everyone he met in the street for news of him, but no one had seen him.

Then he went to look for him at home, and when he got to the door, he knocked.

"Who's there?" asked Lampwick, from inside.

"It's me!" answered the puppet.

"Wait a minute, and I'll open up."

After half an hour the door opened, and you can imagine how surprised Pinocchio was when he entered the room and saw his friend Lampwick with a big cotton cap on his head, pulled all the way down to the tip of his nose.

At the sight of that cap Pinocchio felt almost relieved and immediately thought to himself:

"Maybe my friend is ill with the same illness I have? Maybe he has donkey fever, too?"

And pretending that he hadn't noticed anything, he asked him, smiling:

"How are you, my dear Lampwick?"

"Very well: like a mouse in a wheel of Parmesan cheese."

"Are you really serious?"

"And why should I tell you a lie?"

"Sorry, friend; but then why are you wearing that cotton cap that completely covers your ears?"

"The doctor ordered me to, because I hurt my knee. And you, dear Pinocchio, why are you wearing that cotton cap pulled all the way down to your nose?"

"The doctor ordered me to, because I skinned my foot."

"Oh! Poor Pinocchio!"

"Oh! Poor Lampwick!"

These words were followed by a very long silence, during which the two friends did nothing but look at each other mockingly.

Finally the puppet, with a honeyed and suave voice, said to his friend:

"Satisfy my curiosity, my dear Lampwick: have you ever suffered from an illness of the ears?"

"Never! . . . And you?"

"Never! But since this morning I have had a very painful ear."

"I have the same problem."

"You too? And which is the ear that hurts you?"

"Both of them. And you?"

"Both of them. Could it be the same illness?"

"I'm afraid so."

"Would you do me a favor, Lampwick?"

"Gladly! With all my heart."

"Would you show me your ears?"

"Why not? But first I want to see yours, dear Pinocchio."

"No: you have to be the first."

"No, my dear little fellow! First you, and then me!"

"Well, then," said the puppet, "let's make a friends' agreement."

"Let's hear what this agreement is."

"Let's both take off our caps at the same time. Do you accept?"

"I accept."

"So, then, attention!"

And Pinocchio began to count out loud:

"One! Two! Three!"

At the word "three!" the two boys took their caps off their heads and threw them into the air.

And then something happened that would seem incredible if it weren't true. It happened, that is to say, that Pinocchio and Lampwick, when they saw that they had both been struck by the same misfortune, instead of being mortified and afflicted, started to wiggle their enormously overgrown ears at each other, and after a thousand coarse gestures they ended up breaking into loud laughter.

And they laughed, and laughed, and laughed so hard that they had to hold their sides, until, just as they were laughing the hardest, Lampwick suddenly grew silent, and, staggering and changing color, he said to his friend:

"Help, help, Pinocchio!"

"What's the matter?"

"Oh dear! I can't stand up straight on my legs anymore."

"I can't either," shouted Pinocchio, crying and lurching.

And as they were saying this, they both bent over on all fours, and, walking on their hands and knees, they began to move and then to run about the room. And as they were running, their arms turned into hoofed legs, their faces grew longer and became muzzles, and their backs were covered with a coat that was light gray with black speckles.

But do you know what the most awful moment for those two

E risero, risero, risero da doversi reggere il corpo . . .

wretches was? The most awful and most humiliating moment was when they felt their tails sprout from behind. Overcome at that point by shame and misery, they tried to cry and lament their destiny.

They should never have done so! Instead of moans and laments, they let out asinine braying; and braying sonorously, the two of them sang in chorus: "hee-haw, hee-haw, hee-haw."

In the meantime there was a knock on the door, and a voice outside said:

"Open up! It's the Little Man, the driver of the carriage that brought you to this town. Open up right away, or there will be trouble for you!"

CHAPTER THIRTY-THREE

**After Pinocchio becomes a real little donkey
he is taken to be sold, and the director of a
company of clowns buys him with the
intention of teaching him to dance and
jump hoops. But one evening he becomes
lame, and then someone else buys him
to make a drum out of his skin.**

WHEN HE SAW that the door wasn't opening, the Little Man sent it flying open with a most violent kick, and once he had entered the room, he said to Pinocchio and Lampwick with his usual little laugh:

"Good boys! You brayed well, and I recognized you from your voices right away. And so here I am."

At first the two little donkeys stood there in low spirits, with their heads bowed, their ears flattened, and their tails between their legs.

Initially the Little Man stroked them, petted them, squeezed them; then he pulled out his currycomb and began to brush them down carefully. And when, by force of the brushing, he had gotten them as shiny as two mirrors, he put halters on them and led them to the market square, hoping to sell them and pick up a fair profit.

The buyers, in fact, didn't keep him waiting.

Lampwick was bought by a farmer whose ass had died the day before, and Pinocchio was sold to the director of a company of clowns and acrobats, who bought him with the intention of training him to jump and dance along with the other animals in the company.

And now, my little readers, have you figured out what the Little Man's fine trade was? This horrible little monster, whose appearance was all milk and honey, from time to time would travel through the world with a carriage. Along the way he would use promises and blandishments to gather up all the lazy boys he could find, the ones bored with books and school. And after loading them onto his carriage, he would take them off to "Playland," where they could spend all their time playing games, making a racket, and having fun. When those poor deluded boys, by virtue of playing around all the time and never studying, became so many little donkeys, then he, all cheerful and happy, would become their master and take them to be sold at fairs and markets. And so in just a few years he had made a pretty penny and had become a millionaire.

Whatever happened to Lampwick I do not know. I do know that right from his first days Pinocchio encountered a life that was terribly burdensome and full of hardships.

When he was led to the stable, his new master filled up the manger with straw, but Pinocchio, after tasting a mouthful of it, spit it back out.

Then his master, grumbling, filled the manger with hay, but he didn't like the hay either.

"Ha! You don't like hay either?" shouted his master, agitated. "We'll just see, my dear little donkey; if your head is full of whims, I'll take care of getting rid of them for you!"

And to set him straight he immediately dealt Pinocchio's legs a lash of his whip.

Pinocchio began to cry and bray out of the great pain, and as he brayed he said:

"Hee haw, hee haw, I can't digest straw!"

"So eat the hay!" replied his master, who understood the asinine dialect very well.

"Hee haw, hee haw, hay makes my belly ache!"

"So do you expect me to maintain an ass like you on chicken
breasts and capon galantine?" continued his master, getting more
and more angry and dealing him another lash of the whip.

At that second lash Pinocchio, out of prudence, immediately
fell silent and said nothing else.

Meanwhile the stable had been closed and Pinocchio found
himself alone, and since he hadn't eaten for many hours he began
to yawn out of his great hunger. And yawning, his mouth opened
so wide that it looked like an oven.

Finally, finding nothing else in the manger, he resigned himself to chewing a bit of hay, and after he had chewed it up very
well, he closed his eyes and made it go down.

"This hay isn't bad," he said to himself then, "but how much
better it would have been if I had continued to study! Right now I
could be eating a little piece of fresh bread and a nice slice of
salami! Oh well!"

As soon as he woke up the next morning he looked in the
manger for another bit of hay, but he didn't find any, since he had
eaten it all during the night.

So he took a mouthful of chopped straw; and as he was
chewing it he had to recognize that the taste of chopped straw did
not remotely resemble either a Milanese risotto or Neapolitan
macaroni.

"Oh well!" he repeated, continuing to chew. "At least I hope
that my misfortune may be a lesson to all disobedient children
who don't want to study. Oh well! . . . Oh well!"

"The heck with your oh wells!" shouted his master, coming
into the stable right then. "I suppose you think, my dear little
donkey, that I bought you for the sole purpose of giving you food
and drink? I bought you so that you would work and so that you
would help me earn lots of money. So get up, like a good fellow!
Come with me to the Circus, where I'll teach you to jump hoops,

break paper barrels with your head, and dance the waltz and the polka while standing on your hind legs."

Poor Pinocchio had to learn all these splendid things, whether he liked it or not; but it took him three months of lessons and a good many hide-tanning lashes of the whip to learn them.

The day finally came when his master was able to announce a truly extraordinary show. The many-colored posters plastered on the street corners read:

GRAND GALA PERFORMANCE

This evening
THE USUAL ACROBATICS AND
SURPRISING EXERCISES

will take place

PERFORMED BY ALL THE COMPANY'S ARTISTS
AND BY ALL THE HORSES OF BOTH SEXES

and also

FOR THE FIRST TIME EVER
WE WILL PRESENT THE FAMOUS

LITTLE DONKEY PINOCCHIO

known as

THE STAR OF THE DANCE

 The theater will be illuminated.

On that evening, as you can imagine, the theater was packed full an hour before the show was to begin.

There was neither an orchestra seat, nor a seat in the stalls, nor a box available, not even for its weight in gold.

The tiers of the circus were teeming with little boys, little girls, and older children of all ages who were in a fever of excitement to see the famous little donkey Pinocchio dance.

When the first part of the show was over, the Director of the company, who was dressed in a black jacket, white breeches, and leather boots that went above his knees, presented himself to the huge audience that crowded the theater and, bowing low, recited with great solemnity the following garbled speech:

"Respectable audience, ladies and gentlemen!

"The humble undersigned, while passing through this illustrious metropolitan, wanted to create the honor as well as the pleasure of presenting to this intelligent and substantial public a famous little donkey who has already had the honor of dancing in the presence of His Majesty the emperor of all the principal courts of Europe.

"And while thanking you, please assist us with your animating presence and sympathize with us!"

This speech was received with much laughter and much applause, but the applause doubled and became something of a hurricane at the appearance of the little donkey Pinocchio in the middle of the circus ring. He was decked out in his finest dress. He had a new bridle of shiny leather with brass buckles and studs; two white camellias behind his ears; his mane was divided into a great number of curls, each tied with a little bow of red silk; he had a large belt of gold and silver around his middle; and his tail was all braided with purple and light blue velvet ribbons. He was, in short, a donkey you could fall in love with!

The Director, when he presented Pinocchio to the audience, added these words:

"My respectable auditors! I won't stand here and make mendacity of the great difficulties that I suppressated in order to comprehend and subjugate this mammal, while it was freely grazing from mountain to mountain on the plains of the Torrid Zone. I beg you to observe the wild game transuding from his eyes, and for this very reason and since all the attempts to tame him to live like a civil quadruped have been in vanity, more than once I have had to resort to the affable dialect of the whip. But each gesture of kindness on my part, instead of endearing me to him, has made his spirit even more ill-disposed to me. Following the Wales Method, however, I was able to find a small piece of bony cartilage on his skull, which the Medici School of Paris itself recognized to be the regenerative bulb of hair growth and Pyrrhic dance. And so I decided to give him a training in dance, not to mention the other relative forms of jumping hoops and paper barrels. Admire him! And then judge him! But before I take my leaf of you, allow me, ladies and gentlemen, to invite you to the matinee performance that will be held tomorrow evening. In the apotheosis, however, that rainy weather threatens to rain, then instead of tomorrow evening, the performance will be delayed until tomorrow morning, at 11 A.M. in the afternoon."

And here the Director gave another very low bow. Then, turning to Pinocchio, he said to him:

"Chin up, Pinocchio! Before you begin your exercises, greet this respectable audience, ladies, gentlemen, and children."

Pinocchio, obeying him, immediately bent his two front knees until they touched the ground, and he stayed in this kneeling position until the Director cracked his whip and shouted at him:

"Walk!"

Then the donkey got up on his four legs and began to go around the circus ring, walking faster and faster.

After a while the Director shouted:

"Trot!" and Pinocchio, obeying the command, changed his pace to a trot.

"Gallop!" and Pinocchio broke into a gallop.

"Full speed!" and Pinocchio ran at full speed. But just as he was running like a racehorse, the Director, raising his arm in the air, fired his pistol.

At that shot the little donkey pretended to be wounded, and fell to the ground in the ring, as if he were really dying.

After he had risen from the ground, in the midst of an explosion

"Animo, Pinocchio! Avanti di dar principio ai vostri esercizi, salutate
questo rispettabile pubblico, cavalieri, dame e ragazzi!"

of applause, shouts, and clapping that nearly reached the stars, Pinocchio had the natural urge to lift his head and look up . . . and as he looked he saw, in one of the boxes, a beautiful lady who was wearing a large gold necklace around her neck, on the end of which hung a medallion. On the medallion was painted the portrait of a puppet.

"That's my portrait! . . . That lady is the Fairy," said Pinocchio to himself, recognizing her at once. And as he was overcome by great happiness, he tried to yell:

"Oh, my little Fairy! Oh, my little Fairy!"

But instead of these words, out of his throat came a braying sound that was so sonorous and prolonged that it made all the spectators laugh, and in particular all the children who were present.

Then the Director, in order to teach him a lesson and to make him understand that it's not good manners to start braying in the face of the audience, gave him a blow on the nose with the handle of his whip.

The poor donkey stuck out his tongue a palm's length, and spent at least five minutes licking his nose, perhaps believing that by doing so he would be able to sop up the pain that he was feeling.

But imagine how great his desperation was when, turning to look up a second time, he saw that the box was empty and that the Fairy had disappeared!

He felt like he was dying: his eyes filled with tears and he began to cry uncontrollably. But no one noticed, and least of all the Director, who, cracking his whip, shouted:

"Good boy, Pinocchio! Now you'll show these ladies and gentlemen how gracefully you can jump the hoops."

Pinocchio tried two or three times, but each time he reached the hoop, instead of going through it he found it more comfortable to pass under it. Finally he took a leap and went through it, but unfortunately his hind legs remained tangled in the hoop, for which reason he fell to the ground on the other side, all in a heap.

When he got up, he was limping, and he was barely able to return to the stables.

"Come out, Pinocchio! We want the little donkey! Come out, little donkey!" the children in the stalls shouted, full of pity and touched by the terribly sad event.

But that evening the little donkey was not to be seen again.

The next morning the veterinarian — that is, the animal doctor — declared, after examining him, that he would remain lame for his whole life.

Then the Director said to his stable boy:

"What do you want me to do with a lame jackass? He'd be a good-for-nothing who'd live off me. So take him to the square and sell him again."

When they reached the square, they immediately found a buyer, who asked the stable boy:

"How much do you want for that little lame donkey?"

"Twenty lire."

"I'll give you twenty cents. Don't think that I'm buying him to use him for anything; the only reason I'm buying him is for his skin. I can see he has a very thick skin, and I want to make a drum out of his skin for the town band."

I'll let you imagine, children, what a nice pleasure it was for poor Pinocchio when he heard that he was destined to become a drum!

The fact of the matter is that the buyer, as soon as he had paid the twenty pennies, led the little donkey to the seashore; and after hanging a stone around the donkey's neck and tying his leg to a piece of rope that he held in his hand, he suddenly gave the donkey a big shove and hurled him down into the water.

With that rock around his neck, Pinocchio went straight to the bottom, and the buyer, still holding the rope tight in his hand, sat down on the top of a cliff and waited for the little donkey to have all the time he needed to die of drowning, so that he could then flay him and remove his skin.

CHAPTER THIRTY-FOUR

**After Pinocchio is thrown into the sea
he is eaten by fish and goes back to
being a puppet as he was before. But
as he is swimming to save himself,
he is swallowed by the terrible Shark.**

AFTER THE LITTLE donkey had been underwater for fifty minutes the buyer said, discussing it with himself:

"By now my poor little lame donkey must be good and drowned. Let's pull him up, then, and make a nice drum out of his skin."

And he began to pull the rope that he had tied to the donkey's leg: and he pulled, and pulled, and pulled until . . . can you guess what he finally saw appear on the surface of the water? Instead of a little dead donkey, he saw a live puppet appear on the surface of the water, wriggling like an eel.

When he saw that wooden puppet, the poor man thought he was dreaming and stood there in a daze, his mouth open and his eyes bulging out of his head.

After he had recovered a little from his initial amazement, he said, crying and stuttering:

"And where's the little donkey that I threw into the sea?"

"I'm that little donkey!" answered the puppet, laughing.

"You?"

"Me."

"Ha! You scoundrel! You think you can make fun of me?"

"Make fun of you? Nothing of the sort, my dear master: I'm serious."

"But how come you, who were a little donkey a short while ago, have now, after being in the water, become a wooden puppet?"

"It must be the effect of the seawater. The sea plays these sorts of jokes."

"Watch out, puppet, watch out! Don't think you can amuse yourself behind my back! You'll be in trouble if I lose my patience!"

"All right, then, master; do you want to know the whole true story? Untie this leg for me and I'll tell you."

The buyer, that fine bumbler, was curious to know the true story and immediately untied the knot in the rope to which the puppet was tied. And then Pinocchio, finding himself as free as a bird in the air, began to speak in this manner:

"You should know, then, that I used to be a wooden puppet, like I am today. But I was just a touch away from becoming a boy like so many other boys in this world, except that, due to my half-hearted desire to study and to the fact that I listened to bad companions, I ran away from home . . . and one fine day when I woke up I found myself transformed into a jackass, with ears this long! . . . and a tail this long! . . . What a disgrace that was for me! . . . A disgrace, dear master, that I hope blessed Saint Anthony never has even you experience! When I was taken to the ass market, I was bought by the Director of an equestrian company, who got it into his head to make a great dancer and a great hoop-jumper out of me. But one evening, during the performance, I took a nasty fall in the theater and became lame in both legs. Then the Director, not knowing what to do with a lame ass, sent me off to be sold again, and you bought me!"

"I'm afraid so! And I paid twenty cents for you. So now who's going to give me back my poor twenty cents?"

"And why did you buy me? You bought me to make a drum out of my skin! A drum!"

"I'm afraid so! And now where am I going to find another skin?"

"Don't despair, master. There are lots of little donkeys in this world!"

"Tell me, impertinent rascal: does your story end here?"

"No," answered the puppet, "I've got another couple of words to say, and then I'll be done. After you bought me, you brought me to this place to kill me. But then, giving in to a merciful sentiment of humanity, you preferred to tie a rock to my neck and throw me to the bottom of the sea. This delicate sentiment does you great honor and I'll always be eternally grateful to you for it. This time, however, my dear master, you did your calculations without taking into consideration the Fairy . . ."

"And who is this Fairy?"

"She's my mother, and she's like all good mothers who love their children very much, and never lose sight of them, and take loving care of them through every misfortune, even when these children, because of their thoughtlessness and bad behavior, would deserve to be abandoned and left to fare for themselves. So, as I was saying, as soon as the good Fairy saw that I was in danger of drowning, she immediately sent an enormous school of fish over to me. And believing me really to be a little donkey who was already dead, they began to eat me! And what big mouthfuls they took! I would never have thought that fish were even greedier than children! . . . One of them ate my ears, one my muzzle, one my neck and mane, one the skin on my feet, one the fur on my back . . . and, among the others, there was a little fish that was so polite that it even deigned to eat my tail."

"From today on," said the buyer, horrified, "I swear I'm never going to taste fish again. It would be too unpleasant to open a red mullet or a fried hake and find a donkey tail inside in its stomach!"

"I'm of the same opinion as you," replied the puppet, laughing. "Moreover, you should know that when the fish had finished eating all of the asinine skin that covered me from head to foot, they got to the bone, as is natural. Or, I should say, they

"Dicevo, dunque, che la buona Fata, appena
mi vide in pericolo di affogare . . ."

got to the wood, because as you see I'm made of very hard wood. But after they took the first bites, those greedy fish immediately realized that the wood wasn't meat for their teeth, and, nauseated by this indigestible food, they left, some going this way and some going that way, without even turning around to say thank you. And that's the tale of how, when you pulled up the rope, you found a live puppet instead of a dead little donkey."

"I don't give a hoot for your story," yelled the furious buyer. "All I know is that I spent twenty pennies to buy you, and I want my money back. You know what I'm going to do? I'm going to bring you back to the market, and I'll sell you again for your weight in seasoned wood to use for fireplace kindling."

"Go ahead and sell me again; it's fine with me," said Pinocchio.

But as he was saying this, he took a fine leap and landed with a splash in the water. And as he swam happily away and got farther from the beach, he yelled at the poor buyer:

"Good-bye, master; if you need a skin to make a drum out of, remember me."

The fact of the matter is that in the wink of an eye he was so far away that you could barely see him anymore: that is, all you could see was a little black spot on the surface of the sea, which every now and then thrust its legs out of the water and did somersaults and dives, like a dolphin in a good mood.

While Pinocchio thus swam forth with no certain destination he saw a rock that seemed to be made of white marble in the middle of the sea. And on top of the rock there was a lovely little goat that was bleating affectionately and gesturing to him to come closer.

The most singular thing was this: that the little goat's wool, instead of being white, or black, or with spots of various colors, like other goats' wool, was, instead, all blue, but a blue so radiant that it brought very much to mind the lovely Little Girl's hair.

I'll let you wonder if poor Pinocchio's heart started to beat harder! Doubling his strength and energy he began to swim toward the white rock, and he was already halfway there when all of a sudden the horrible head of a sea monster came out of the water and started moving toward him, with its mouth gaping open like a pit and three rows of huge teeth that would have been frightening even if they had only been painted in a picture.

And do you know who that sea monster was?

That sea monster was none other than the gigantic Shark that has been mentioned a number of times in this story, the one that on account of his massacres and his insatiable voracity had been given the nickname of "the Attila of fish and fishermen."

Imagine poor Pinocchio's fear at the sight of the monster. He tried to dodge him, to change direction; he tried to escape; but that immense gaping mouth kept on coming toward him with the speed of an arrow.

"Hurry up, Pinocchio, for goodness' sake!" yelled the lovely little goat, bleating.

And Pinocchio swam in desperation, with his arms, with his chest, with his legs and his feet.

"Move fast, Pinocchio; the monster's getting closer!"

And Pinocchio, gathering all his strength, doubled his efforts to race away.

"Watch out, Pinocchio! . . . The monster's catching up with you! . . . Here he is! . . . Here he is! . . . Hurry up, for goodness' sake, or you're done for!"

And Pinocchio swam more swiftly than ever, away, away, away, as fast as a rifle bullet. And he was already nearing the rock, and the little goat, hanging out over the sea, was already holding out her front legs to help him get out of the water! . . . But!

But at that point it was too late! The monster had caught up with him. The monster, sucking in his breath, drank the poor puppet right up, like he would have drunk a fresh chicken's egg, and he swallowed him so violently and so greedily that Pinocchio, falling down into the Shark's stomach, received such a rude blow that he remained dazed for a quarter of an hour.

Even when he came back to his senses after being stunned like that, he wasn't able to figure out what sort of world he was in. Sur-

"... Eccolo! ... Eccolo! ..."

rounding him was a vast darkness that went in every direction: a darkness that was so black and deep that he felt like he had stuck his head into an inkwell full of ink. He stopped and listened and didn't hear a sound; the only things he felt were a few big gusts of wind that hit him in the face from time to time. He wasn't able, initially, to determine where that wind was coming from, but then he realized that it was coming from the monster's lungs. Because, you see, the Shark suffered terribly from asthma, and when he breathed, it was just as if the north wind were blowing.

At first, Pinocchio did all he could to gather up a little courage. But when he had proof and then even more proof that he was shut inside the sea monster's stomach he began to cry and to shriek, and as he cried he said:

"Help! Help! Oh, poor me! Isn't there anyone who's going to come and save me?"

"Who do you expect to save you, you wretch?" said, out of that darkness, an awful, cracked voice that sounded like an out-of-tune guitar.

"Who's talking like that?" asked Pinocchio, feeling his blood chill with fear.

"It's me! I'm a poor Tuna, who was swallowed by the Shark along with you. And what type of fish are you?"

"I have nothing to do with fish. I'm a puppet."

"Well then, if you're not a fish, why did you let yourself be swallowed by the monster?"

"I wasn't the one that let myself be swallowed; he's the one that swallowed me! And now what are we supposed to do here in the dark?"

"Resign ourselves and wait for the Shark to digest both of us!"

"But I don't want to be digested!" howled Pinocchio, starting to cry again.

"I wouldn't like to be digested, either," continued the Tuna, "but I'm something of a philosopher and I gain comfort from the thought that when you're born a Tuna, there's more dignity in dying underwater than in oil!"

"Nonsense!" yelled Pinocchio.

"That's my opinion," replied the Tuna, "and opinions, as political Tunas say, must be respected!"

"The fact of the matter is . . . I want to get out of here . . . I want to escape . . ."

"Escape, if you can!"

"Is this Shark that swallowed us very big?" asked the puppet.

"Calculate that his body is more than half a mile long, not counting the tail."

As they were having this conversation in the dark, Pinocchio seemed to see a sort of glimmer far, far away.

"Whatever can that little light be, so far, far away?" said Pinocchio.

"It must be one of our companions in misfortune who's waiting to be digested, like us!"

"I want to go and find him. Couldn't it perhaps be some old fish who would be able to show me the way to escape?"

"I hope with all my heart that it is, dear puppet."

"Good-bye, Tuna."

"Good-bye, puppet, and good luck."

"Where will we see each other again?"

"Who knows? . . . It's better not to even think about that!"

CHAPTER THIRTY-FIVE

**In the Shark's belly Pinocchio again meets
up with . . . who does he meet up with?
Read this chapter and you'll find out.**

As soon as Pinocchio had said good-bye to his good friend Tuna he stumbled forward in that darkness, and, groping his way along the Shark's belly, he directed his steps one after the other toward that little glimmer that he saw flickering far, far away.

And as he walked he felt his feet splashing in a puddle of greasy, slippery water, and that water smelled so strongly of fried fish that it seemed to him that he was in the middle of Lent.

And the farther he went, the brighter and clearer the light became, until, after walking and walking, he finally arrived. And when he had arrived . . . what did he find? You'd never in a thousand years guess: he found a little set table, and on it was a burning candle stuck in a green glass bottle, and sitting at the table was a little old man who was completely white, as if he were made of snow or whipped cream, and who was busy chewing on some little fish that were still alive — so alive, in fact, that at times, as he was eating them, they would actually jump out of his mouth.

At this sight Pinocchio felt such great and unexpected happiness that he came quite close to falling into a frenzy. He wanted to laugh, he wanted to cry, he wanted to say a great many things. Instead he mumbled in a confused way and stammered out a few broken-off and incoherent words. He finally managed to let out a shout of joy and, opening his arms wide and throwing them around the neck of the little old man, he began to shout:

"Oh, my dear little Father! I've finally found you! Now I'm never going to leave you again, never ever again!"

"Can I really believe my eyes, then?" replied the little old man, rubbing his eyes. "So you're really my dear Pinocchio?"

"Yes, yes, it's me, it's really me! And you've already forgiven me, haven't you? Oh, little Father, how good you are! And to think that I, on the other hand . . . Oh! But if you only knew how many misfortunes I've been showered with and how many things have gone wrong for me! Just imagine: The day that you, poor little Father, sold your jacket to buy me the spelling book so I could go to school, I ran away to see the puppet show, and the puppet master wanted to put me on the fire so that I could cook his roast mutton, and he was the one who gave me five gold coins, later, so that I could bring them to you; but I came upon the Fox and the Cat, who took me to the Red Lobster Inn, where they ate like wolves, and after I left by myself at night I met the assassins, who began to run after me, and I ran off, and they ran after me, and I ran some more and they still ran after me, and I ran some more, until they hung me on a branch of the Great Oak, where the lovely Little Girl with the blue hair sent a coach to get me, and when the doctors had examined me they immediately said: 'If he's not dead, it's a sign that he's still alive,' and then I let a lie slip out, and my nose started to grow and I could no longer fit it through the door of the room, which is why I went with the Fox and the Cat to bury the four gold coins, since I had spent one at the tavern, and the Parrot started laughing, and instead of two thousand coins there was nothing left, for which the judge, when he heard that I had been robbed, immediately had me put in prison, to satisfy the thieves, and when I left, I saw a fine bunch of grapes in a field, so I got caught in a trap and the farmer, with good reason, put a dog collar on me so that I would guard the chicken coop, and he recognized

"Oh! babbino mio! finalmente vi ho ritrovato!
Ora poi non vi lascio più, mai più, mai più!"

my innocence and let me go, and the Serpent, with his smoking tail, started to laugh and burst a vein in his chest, and so I returned to the house of the lovely Little Girl, who was dead, and the Pigeon, seeing that I was crying, said to me: 'I saw your father building a little boat to go out in search of you,' and I said to him: 'Oh, if only I had wings, too,' and he said to me: 'Do you want to go to where your father is?' and I said to him: 'I wish! But who's going to take me there?' and he said to me: 'I'll take you there,' and I said to him: 'How?' and he said to me: 'Get up on my back,' and so we flew the whole night, and then the next morning all the fishermen who were looking toward the sea said to me: 'There's a poor man in a little boat who's about to drown,' and from far off I immediately recognized you, because my heart told me so, and I signaled to you to come back to the beach . . ."

"I recognized you, too," said Geppetto, "and I would gladly have returned to the beach, but how could I? The sea was rough and a huge wave capsized my boat. Then, as soon as he saw me in the water, a horrible Shark that was nearby came right for me, and he stuck his tongue out, sucked me neatly in, and swallowed me as if I were a Bologna tortellino."

"And how long is it that you've been shut up in here?" asked Pinocchio.

"It must be two years now, since that day. Two years, my Pinocchio, that have seemed like two centuries to me!"

"And how were you able to survive? And where did you find the candle? And the matches to light it, who gave them to you?"

"I'll tell you the whole story now. You should know, then, that the same storm that capsized my little boat also sunk a merchant ship. The sailors all survived, but the ship sunk to the bottom, and after swallowing me the Shark, who had an excellent appetite that day, swallowed the ship, too . . ."

"What? He swallowed it in one bite?" asked Pinocchio, amazed.

"All in one bite; the only thing he spit out was the main mast, since it got stuck in his teeth like a fish bone. To my great luck that ship was loaded with canned meat packed in tin boxes, but also biscuits — that is, toasted bread — bottles of wine, raisins, cheese, coffee, sugar, tallow candles, and boxes of wax matches. With all of this grace of God I've been able to survive for two years, but today I'm down to my last drop: today there's nothing left in the cupboard, and this candle, which you see lit, is the last candle I have . . ."

"And then what?"

"And then, my dear, we'll both be left in the dark."

"Well, then, my little Father," said Pinocchio, "there's no time to lose. We've got to think immediately about getting away . . ."

"Getting away? And how?"

"We'll escape through the Shark's mouth, throw ourselves into the sea, and swim off."

"That makes fine sense, but I, dear Pinocchio, don't know how to swim."

"And what does that matter? You'll ride piggyback on my shoulders; I'm a good swimmer and I'll get you to the beach safe and sound."

"Don't delude yourself, my boy!" replied Geppetto, shaking his head and smiling in a melancholy way. "Does it seem possible to you that a puppet who's barely three feet tall, like you, can be strong enough to carry me on his shoulders, swimming?"

"Try it and you'll see! In any case, if it's written in the stars that we have to die, at least we'll have the great comfort of dying in each other's arms."

And without saying another word, Pinocchio took the candle in his hand, and going first so that he could light the way, he said to his father:

"Follow behind me, and don't be afraid."

And they walked like that for a good while, and they crossed the whole belly and the whole body of the Shark. But when they had reached the point where the spacious throat of the monster began, they had the good idea of stopping to take a look at things and waiting for the right moment to escape.

Now, you should know that since the Shark was very old and

suffered from asthma and heart palpitations he was forced to sleep with his mouth open. For this reason Pinocchio, leaning out from the bottom of the throat and looking up, was able to see, above that enormous, wide-open mouth, a lovely piece of starry sky and some splendid moonlight.

"This is the right moment to escape," he whispered then, turning to his father. "The Shark is sleeping like a dormouse; the sea is calm and it's as light as day. Come, then, little Father; follow me and we'll soon be safe."

No sooner said than done. They climbed up the sea monster's throat and when they had reached that enormous mouth, they began to walk on tiptoes across the tongue: a tongue so wide and so long that it looked like a garden lane. And they were just about to take the great leap and throw themselves into the sea and swim off when, right at that very moment, the Shark sneezed, and when he sneezed he gave such a violent jolt that Pinocchio and Geppetto were thrown back and once again sent flying to the bottom of the monster's stomach.

The great impact of the fall put the candle out, and father and son were left in the dark.

"Now what?" asked Pinocchio, becoming serious.

"Now, my boy, we're really done for."

"Why done for? Give me your hand, little Father, and be careful not to slip!"

"Where are you taking me?"

"We have to try to escape again. Come with me and don't be afraid."

Having said this, Pinocchio took his father by the hand, and still walking on tiptoes, together they climbed up the monster's throat again. They crossed the whole tongue and stepped over the three rows of teeth. But before they took the great leap, the puppet said to his father:

"Ride piggyback on my shoulders, and hug me as tight as you can. I'll take care of the rest."

As soon as Geppetto had settled himself comfortably on his

son's shoulders, the good Pinocchio, sure of what he was doing, threw himself into the water and began to swim. The sea was as calm as oil; the moon shone in all its brilliance and the Shark continued to sleep so soundly that even a cannon shot wouldn't have awakened him.

CHAPTER THIRTY-SIX

Pinocchio finally stops being
a puppet and becomes a boy.

$\mathcal{W}$HILE PINOCCHIO was swimming quickly to reach the beach, he realized that his father, who was riding piggyback and had his legs half in the water, was shivering quite violently, as if he had been overcome by a tertian fever.

Was he shivering from cold or from fright? Who knows? Maybe a little of one and a little of the other. But Pinocchio, thinking that it was a shiver of fear, tried to comfort him by saying:

"Take heart, Father! In a few minutes we'll get to land and we'll be safe."

"But where is this blessed beach?" asked the little old man, getting more and more restless, and squinting his eyes, like tailors do when they thread a needle. "Here I am, looking in every direction, and I see nothing but sky and sea."

"But I can see the beach, too," said the puppet. "For your information, I'm like a cat: I see better at night than during the day."

Poor Pinocchio was pretending to be in a good mood. But instead . . . instead he was beginning to get discouraged. He was losing his strength, he was starting to get out of breath and to pant . . . in short, he was worn out, and the beach was still far away.

He swam as long as he still had breath; then he turned his head toward Geppetto, and said, with broken words:

"My dear Father . . . you'll have to help yourself . . . because I'm dying! . . ."

And father and son were on the verge of drowning when they heard a voice like an untuned guitar that said:

"Who is it that's dying?"

"It's me and my poor father!"

"I recognize this voice! You're Pinocchio!"

"Precisely. And who are you?"

"I'm the Tuna, your prisonmate inside the Shark's belly."

"And how did you manage to escape?"

"I imitated your example. You're the one who showed me the route, and after you, I got away, too."

"My dear Tuna, you've showed up just at the right time! I beg of you, for the love that you have for your children the little Tunas: help us, or else we're done for."

"Gladly and with all my heart. Grab onto my tail, both of you, and let me pull you along. In four minutes I'll get you to the beach."

As you can imagine, Geppetto and Pinocchio accepted the offer immediately, but instead of grabbing on to his tail, they thought it would be more comfortable to actually sit on the Tuna's back.

"Are we too heavy?" asked Pinocchio.

"Heavy? Not a chance. It feels like I have two seashells on my back," answered the Tuna, who had a build that was so big and robust that he looked like a two-year-old calf.

When they had reached the shore, Pinocchio jumped to the ground first, so that he could help his father to do the same. Then he turned to the Tuna and, with a voice that showed his emotion, said:

"My friend, you saved my father! And I can't find the right words to thank you enough! At least allow me to give you a kiss as a sign of my eternal gratitude!"

The Tuna stuck his snout out of the water, and Pinocchio, leaning down with his knees on the ground, planted a very affectionate kiss on his mouth. At this show of spontaneous and heartfelt tenderness the poor Tuna, who wasn't used to such things, felt so moved that, ashamed to be seen crying like a child, he plunged his head back into the water.

In the meantime, it had become day.

Then Pinocchio, offering his arm to Geppetto, who had barely enough breath to stand on his own feet, said to him:

"Go ahead, lean on my arm, dear little Father, and let's go. We'll walk very slowly, like ants, and when we're tired we'll rest along the roadside."

"And where should we go?" asked Geppetto.

"In search of a house or a hut where they might be charitable enough to give us a bite of bread and a little straw that we can use as a bed."

They hadn't yet gone a hundred steps when they saw, sitting on the side of the road, two ugly mugs who looked as if they were begging.

They were the Cat and the Fox, but it was impossible to recognize them as what they had once been. Imagine that the Cat, with all his pretending that he was blind, had ended up really going blind, and the Fox, looking very old, had ringworm and was all eaten away on one side of his body; he didn't even have a tail anymore. So goes it. That wicked little thief, having fallen into the most squalid misery, found himself forced one fine day to sell even his splendid tail to a traveling salesman, who bought it to make a flyswatter.

"Oh, Pinocchio!" cried the Fox, in a whiny voice, "show a little charity toward these two poor invalids."

"Invalids!" repeated the Cat.

"Good-bye tricksters," answered the puppet. "You fooled me once, and you're not getting me again."

"You've got to believe us, Pinocchio; today we really are poor and wretched!"

"Wretched!" repeated the cat.

"If you're poor, you deserve it. Remember the proverb that says: 'Stolen money never bears fruit.' Good-bye, tricksters!"

"Have pity on us!"

"On us!"

"Good-bye, tricksters! Remember the proverb that says: 'The devil's flour always makes bad bread.' "

"Don't abandon us!"

"Us!" repeated the Cat.

"Good-bye, tricksters! Remember the proverb that says: 'He who steals the shirt off his neighbor's back, usually dies shirtless.' "

And speaking in this manner, Pinocchio and Geppetto continued calmly on their way until, after they had gone another hundred steps, they saw, at the end of a path that ran through the fields, a pretty hut all made of straw, with a roof covered with bricks and tiles.

"Someone must live in that hut," said Pinocchio. "Let's go over and knock."

And so they went and knocked on the door.

"Who is it?" asked a little voice from within.

"It's a poor father and a poor son, without bread and without a roof over our heads," answered the puppet.

"Turn the key and the door will open," said the same little voice.

Pinocchio turned the key, and the door opened. As soon as they got inside, they looked this way, they looked that way, and they didn't see anyone.

"So where's the owner of the hut?" said Pinocchio, surprised.

"Here I am, up here!"

Father and son immediately looked up toward the ceiling, and on top of a beam they saw the Talking Cricket.

"Oh, my dear little Cricket!" said Pinocchio, greeting him politely.

"Now you call me your 'dear little Cricket,' do you? But do you remember when you threw the handle of a hammer at me, to drive me out of your house?"

"You're right, little Cricket! Drive me out, too . . . throw the handle of a hammer at me, too, but have pity on my poor father . . ."

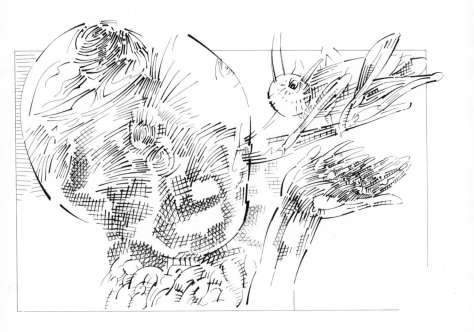

"Oh! mio caro Grillino."

"I'll have pity on the father and on the son, too, but I wanted to remind you of the rude way you treated me in order to teach you that, when it's possible, in this world we have to be kind to everyone if we want to be repaid with equal kindness when we need it."

"You're right, little Cricket, you're absolutely right, and I'll keep in mind the lesson that you've taught me. But will you tell me how you were able to buy this lovely hut?"

"This hut was given to me as a present yesterday by a gracious goat whose wool was a lovely blue color."

"And where did the goat go?" asked Pinocchio, with the keenest curiosity.

"I don't know."

"And when will she come back?"

"She'll never come back. She left yesterday, terribly grief-stricken, and as she was bleating, it seemed that she was saying:

'Poor Pinocchio . . . now I'll never see him again . . . the Shark has probably already eaten him up by now!' "

"She really said that? . . . It was her, then! . . . it was her! . . . it was my dear little Fairy!" Pinocchio began to shout, sobbing and crying uncontrollably.

When he had cried for a good long time, he dried his eyes, and after preparing a nice little bed of straw, he stretched old Geppetto out on it. The he asked the Talking Cricket:

"Tell me, little Cricket: where might I find a glass of milk for my poor father?"

"Three fields over from here lives the vegetable farmer Giangio, who keeps cows. Go to him and you'll find the milk you're looking for."

Pinocchio ran to the house of Giangio the vegetable farmer, but the farmer said to him:

"How much milk do you want?"

"I want a full glass."

"A glass of milk costs one cent. So start by giving me the cent."

"I don't have even half a cent," answered Pinocchio, terribly mortified and sad.

"That's bad, my puppet!" replied the farmer. "If you don't have even a cent, I don't have even a finger of milk."

"Oh well!" said Pinocchio, and he made as if to leave.

"Wait a minute," said Giangio. "You and I can work something out. Do you want to learn how to turn the waterwheel?"

"What's the waterwheel?"

"It's that wooden instrument that's used to pull water up from the cistern to water the vegetables."

"I'll try . . ."

"So, then, pull up a hundred pails of water for me and I'll give you a glass of milk as your payment."

"All right."

Giangio took the puppet into the vegetable garden and taught him how to turn the waterwheel. Pinocchio immediately set to work, but before he had pulled up the hundred pails of water he was completely drenched with sweat from head to toe. He had never endured such hard work.

"Up until now," said the vegetable farmer, "I've always had my little donkey do this job of turning the waterwheel, but today that poor animal is at the end of his life."

"Would you take me to see him?" said Pinocchio.

"Gladly."

As soon as Pinocchio entered the barn he saw a lovely little donkey lying on the straw, worn out by hunger and too much work. When he had stared at him for a good long while, he said to himself, getting agitated:

"And yet, I know that little donkey! His face is not new to me!"

And bending down to him, he asked him in asinine dialect:

"Who are you?"

At this question, the little donkey opened his dying eyes, and answered, stuttering, in the same dialect:

"I'm Lamp . . . wick . . ."

And then he closed his eyes again and breathed his last.

"Oh! Poor Lampwick!" said Pinocchio in a low voice, and he took a handful of straw and dried a tear that was trickling down his face.

"You're so touched by an ass that didn't cost you anything?" said the vegetable farmer. "What am I supposed to do, then, I who bought him with cold cash?"

"I'll tell you . . . he was a friend of mine!"

"A friend of yours?"

"A schoolmate of mine!"

"What?" howled Giangio, breaking into loud laughter. "What?! You had jackasses for schoolmates? I can just imagine the wonderful schoolwork you must have done!"

Feeling mortified by those words, the puppet didn't answer, but he took his glass of lukewarm milk and went back to the hut.

And from that day on, for more than five months he continued to get up every morning before dawn so that he could go and turn the waterwheel and thus earn that glass of milk that was so beneficial to

E dopo richiuse gli occhi e spirò.

the delicate health of his father. Nor did he content himself with this, since in his free time he also learned how to make baskets and hampers of rush. And with the money that he made he took care of all their daily expenses in a most sensible way. Among other things he built, all by himself, an elegant little wheelchair, so that he could take his father out for walks on nice days and let him get a breath of fresh air.

And in the evenings, he practiced reading and writing. In the nearby town he had bought a big book, which was missing its frontispiece and index, for a few cents; he did his reading with this book. As far as writing went, he used a sharpened twig as a pen, and since he had neither inkwell nor ink, he dipped it into a little bottle full of blackberry and cherry juice.

The fact of the matter is that because of his strong will to do his very best, to work, and to eke out a living, not only did he manage to support almost comfortably his parent, who was still a bit ill, but what's more, he was even able to put aside forty coins to buy himself a new little outfit.

One morning he said to his father:

"I'm going to the market nearby to buy myself a little jacket, a little cap, and a pair of shoes. When I get back home," he continued, laughing, "I'll be dressed so well that you'll mistake me for a great gentleman."

And he went out of the house and started to run off, all happy and full of joy. Then all of a sudden he heard someone calling his name, and as he turned he saw a pretty snail coming out from a hedge.

"Don't you recognize me?" said the Snail.

"I seem to, and don't seem to . . ."

"Don't you remember that Snail who worked as a maid for the blue-haired Fairy? Don't you recall that time when I came down to bring you a light and you ended up with a foot stuck in the front door?"

"I remember it all," yelled Pinocchio. "Answer me this minute, my pretty little Snail: where did you last see my good

Fairy? What is she doing? Has she forgiven me? Does she still remember me? Does she still love me? Is she very far from here?
Could I go and see her?"

All these questions that Pinocchio asked so impetuously, without
even stopping to take a breath, were answered by the Snail with her
usual calm:

"My dear Pinocchio! The poor Fairy is lying in a bed at the
hospital!"

"At the hospital?"

"I'm afraid so. After she was struck by a thousand misfortunes,
she fell gravely ill and no longer has enough to buy herself even a
bite of bread."

"Really? Oh! What terrible sorrow you've caused me! Oh!
Poor little Fairy! Poor little Fairy! Poor little Fairy! . . . If I had a
million, I'd run and bring it to her . . . But all I have are forty coins
. . . Here they are: I was just going to buy myself a new outfit. Take
them, Snail, and go give them to my good Fairy right away."

"And your new outfit?"

"What do I care about the new outfit? I would even sell the
rags I'm wearing to help her! Go, Snail, and make it quick, and in
two days come back here, because I hope to be able to give you a
few more coins. Up till now I've been working to support my father; from today on, I'll work an extra five hours each day to support my good mother, too. Good-bye, Snail, and I'll be waiting for
you in two days."

The Snail, as was not her habit, darted off like a lizard in the
dog days of August.

When Pinocchio got back home, his father asked him:

"And your new outfit?"

"I wasn't able to find one that fit well. Never mind! I'll buy it
some other time."

That evening Pinocchio, instead of staying up until ten, stayed
up until well after midnight; and instead of making eight rush baskets, he made sixteen.

Then he went to bed and fell asleep. And as he was sleeping, he thought he saw the Fairy in a dream. She was quite beautiful and smiled at him; after giving him a kiss she said the following:

"Well done, Pinocchio! Thanks to your good heart, I forgive you all the mischief you've gotten into up to now. Children who lovingly help their parents when they are in trouble and when they are ill always deserve great praise and great affection, even if they can't be cited as models of obedience and good behavior. Use good judgment in the future, and you'll be happy."

At this point the dream ended, and Pinocchio woke up, his eyes opened wide in amazement.

Now imagine his astonishment when, upon awakening, he realized that he was no longer a wooden puppet, but that instead he had become a boy just like any other boy. He took a look around, and instead of the usual straw walls of the hut he saw a lovely little room that was furnished and decorated with an almost elegant simplicity. Jumping down from the bed he found a fine new set of clothes, a new cap, and a pair of leather boots prepared for him, in which he looked picture perfect.

As soon as he was dressed he had the natural urge to put his hands in his pockets, and he pulled out a little ivory change purse, on which these words were written: "The blue-haired Fairy is paying Pinocchio back for his forty coins, and she thanks him very much for his good heart." When he opened the wallet, instead of the forty copper coins, forty brand-new gold coins lay there shining.

Then he went to look at himself in the mirror, and he looked like someone else. He no longer saw the usual image of the wooden marionette reflected there, but he saw the lively and intelligent image of a handsome young lad with brown hair, blue eyes, and as happy and gay an air as if he were in heaven.

In the midst of all these marvelous things, which were following one upon the other, Pinocchio himself no longer knew whether he was really awake or whether he was still dreaming, this time with his eyes open.

"And where's my father?" he yelled, all of a sudden, and when

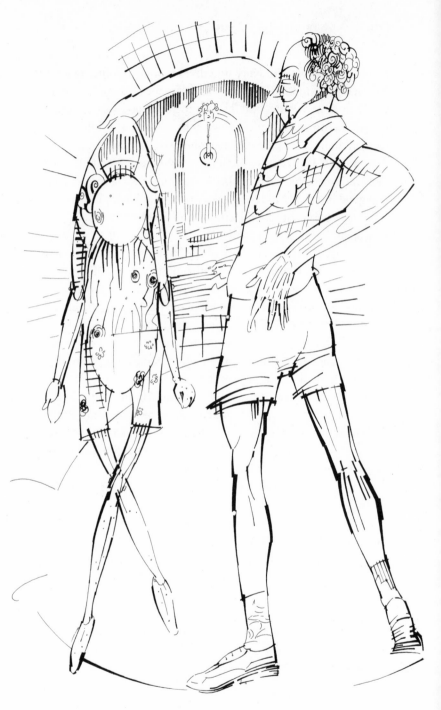

"Com'ero buffo, quand'ero un burattino!"

he entered the room next to his he found Geppetto healthy, spry, and in a good mood, just as he had once been. He had immediately taken up his profession of wood carver again and at that very moment was designing a splendid frame filled with leaves, flowers, and little heads of various animals.

"Just out of curiosity, little Father: what's the reason for all of these sudden changes?" asked Pinocchio, jumping into his arms and showering him with kisses.

"This sudden change in our home is all thanks to you," said Geppetto.

"Why all thanks to me?"

"Because when children go from being bad to good, they have the power to instill a new and cheerful air in their families, too."

"And where do you think the old wooden Pinocchio is hiding?"

"There he is, over there," answered Geppetto, and he pointed to a big puppet propped up against a chair, with its head turned to one side, its arms dangling, and its legs crossed and bent in the middle, so that it seemed a miracle that it even stood up at all.

Pinocchio turned to look at it, and after he had looked at it for a while he said to himself with tremendous satisfaction:

"How funny I was when I was a puppet! And how happy I am now that I've become a respectable boy!"